Dead Before Co-Ed

Mary Vecellio

CARDINAL
HOUND
PRESS

ISBN: 979-8-9913233-4-5

Published by Cardinal Hound Press

"The real danger is not the one who knows he is a monster,

but the one who thinks he is a hero.

Evil is not a distant enemy.

It lives in every human heart.

Waiting for an excuse."

To the silence that wouldn't leave me and the strange path that led me here. I wouldn't trade it for the world.

Chapter One

It's been years, and she finally fucking answered. I snake my car between these ancient mountains, mind looping, stripped raw. I keep turning over the reasons she stayed silent for so long. In just an hour, I'll see Sylvia again—at Discordia's College for Women. It doesn't feel real. I keep asking myself: does she still like me? Has she moved on? Who is she now, and what—if anything—is left of what we were?

I shove those thoughts aside and focus on the road. Doesn't matter. I'm going, and that's that.

Frost clung to the sharp, vivid foliage like some delicate, dying thing. For a moment, I saw my place in the world for what it was. Tiny, microscopic. The Appalachians could swallow me whole without a sound.

I used to think I was different. Special. In Harlowe, South Carolina, that wasn't hard. Surrounded by empty smiles and smaller dreams, I could pretend I was above it. The girls I grew up with shrank into smaller lives year by year. Their boyfriends' lifted trucks were worth more than their futures. I needed more than that.

That fantasy didn't last past graduation. It cracked

under the glare of fluorescent diner lights and the same tired faces, grinding down whatever dreams I'd clung to. I stayed close to home, telling myself I could bloom anywhere. I know better now. No one's exceptional. We're all rooted in the same rotting soil.

But I'll be damned if I let that be me.

Before I left, Mother interrupted my spiraling, like always. "You know we can't force Syl to come down for fall break," her slow Southern drawl heavy with unspoken warnings. "Thought you were dying to get out of this house."

"I am," I replied, trying to sound convinced. "I'm just... not thrilled about meeting her friends. What if it all falls apart?"

She tapped my shoulder twice, meaning she thought she was being profound. "Don't overthink it. Worst case, you fight and come home early."

"Right," I muttered, unsure how that helped anything.

I packed, tried to ignore the weight pressing down on my ribs. I hadn't even left yet and already felt home tugging me back.

The sky opened up as I drove, and the world stretched wide again. I passed a strange mountain, its twin peaks rising like something suggestive from a dream I barely remembered. Sylvia's face drifted into my mind. I'd spent the past week combing through old photos, wondering if she'd changed—or if I was just the one left behind.

Suddenly, I was navigating Discordia's one-way maze—cobblestones, confusion, and history. The streets belonged to another era, though the skyline loomed in the distance. Discordia clung to its bones. Stone and brick, weathered and stubborn. Trees lined the sidewalks, their roots splitting it open attempting to break free. Each bump in the road a reminder of how easily things could fall apart.

I passed a woman in heels and couldn't stop myself from picturing her face-planting into the cracks, bleeding into the cobblestones.

Slowing down, I took in the ivy crawling up old walls, the white picket fences that once corralled horses, and benches scattered like forgotten afterthoughts. The campus was an archive of something half-alive, slowly dissolving.

Finally, I pulled up to a hulking brick building, stone steps leading to thick white Corinthian columns. Through antique windows, I glimpsed staff hunched over desks, trapped in their routines. The road narrowed as I approached Sylvia's dorm. Cemetery Road. Fitting. I was already dying to go home.

My heart slammed against my chest. After all these years, Sylvia was minutes away. Too late to turn back.

***

Her building looked like a row of abandoned townhomes—peeling paint, warped siding. You'd think the place had been deserted if not for the packed lot behind it. Since fall break hadn't started, parking was a nightmare. I left my car in a cracked lot across the street. I didn't grab my things. Just in case.

The wind tangled my copper hair as I crossed the

street. I brushed it out of my face and squared myself before apartment C. The Flats looked like they'd been exiled from campus—three stories of unease. It waited like a predator that didn't need to chase you. I stepped up to the bay window to get a peek into the living room, but the windows were dusted with pollen that hadn't been washed. Each step onto the porch creaked and groaned making a board jut out of place. I could hear Mother's voice echoing faintly; half encouragement, half concern. That passive judgment clung to my thoughts as I stepped onto the porch. I looked up, half in prayer that this was the right place and to make sure the dangling light fixture squeaking in the breeze wasn't going to impale my skull.

I paused, bracing myself as my hand hovered over the doorbell, straining to hear something. The porch swing clinked its chains in the lazy breeze.

Five rings. Five minutes. No answer.

I stepped back and looked up at the narrow mansard windows. Still nothing. I bit my lip, unsure if I should wait or bail. My feet decided for me, carrying me toward the tree-lined path. To the left, the city buzzed. To the right, a shaded walkway bent toward campus. I tried calling Sylvia, straight to voicemail—maybe she was in class—but I wasn't going to sit there and rot.

My mind tugged toward campus, but my body turned the other way—into the cemetery just across the path. The headstones were modest, unmoving. The world outside rushed past, but here, everything paused. The white arch at the entrance gleamed in the sunlight, gold lettering catching between the branches:

AND THE SHADOWS FLEE AWAY.

I wandered through the neat rows of marble, each step easing the tension in my chest. Living in the moment had always been my greatest challenge, as though time was too slippery to hold onto. But here, in the stillness, my thoughts could stretch out. There was clarity in the monotony of these spaces—tragically beautiful, incomprehensible, yet grounding.

The memory of freshman year hit me again like it always did in places like this. Freshman year. A school trip. Me, curled around a toilet, ears ringing, skin buzzing. My body betraying me when the world spun too fast. It was terrifying. But in a way, that disconnection was power. I learned to find my footing in chaos.

That same quiet panic curled at the edges of my thoughts as I wandered deeper into the cemetery. But this time, it felt different. The white stones anchored me—like puzzle pieces I hadn't figured out yet. Something in the air, or the way light angled through the branches, felt like it was reaching for me. I imagined laying my thoughts down here. Letting them stay outside of me, where they couldn't gnaw. The peace felt real—but fragile. Fleeting.

Then I saw her.

Near a mausoleum, a woman stood alone. Her fiery hair blazed in the fading light—almost identical to mine. The color jolted me. She looked like she belonged here, carved from shadow and stone. She stared like she knew me.

Our eyes met. My chest clenched. I raised a hand, tentative. She smiled—barely, just a flicker—but it sent a chill up my spine. Something about it, or her, or the way she held herself, tugged at something buried deep.

And then—she vanished. Back into the shadows. Smoke dissolving into the dusk.

Chapter Two

The sweet, savory scent of rosemary and cinnamon pulled me toward a rickety door with an eighteenth-century latch. Above it hung a wooden sign carved with a Danish whisk and the word "Bakery." I knew I'd found the place.

Inside, the smell wrapped around me—warm, heady, and intoxicating. Shelves groaned under the weight of artisan breads, cookies, cakes, jams, and jellies. I locked eyes on a loaf of rosemary garlic bread and snatched it from the brittle wooden shelf like buried treasure.

That mix of wood, pine, and peppery warmth transported me to a comforting place. I clung to that small comfort now, trying to stay grounded amidst the narrow, crowded shop.

An elderly woman behind the counter smiled wide. "Sugar Cake Popcorn, dear?"

I nodded and handed her my money while another cashier loaded my haul into a hand-stamped paper bag.

I left with my bag heavy as I wandered toward the square. I noticed a white picket fence that led into the center of the campus. As I made my way, my mind drifted to Syl.

"No." I shook my head, pushing the thought away. "Get out of my head." This isn't the time for introspection. "Live in the moment, Edith."

I swallowed the thought, blaming it on hunger or road weariness. The campus felt dead, though the timing suggested classes should be letting out. The bell tower chimed faintly from the church a few buildings over. I glanced at my phone: 3:25. Not exactly a rush hour of students. My paranoia flared.

I followed the pristine path to the school's crest inlaid in concrete. A small courtyard had tables shaded with umbrellas—perfect enough. I shot Sylvia a text, described where I was, and sat down. Unwrapping the warm loaf, the first bite hit hard: rosemary, garlic, and just enough salt. I laughed aloud. Maybe Mother was right. I needed to stop overthinking.

I said it in my head, but the moment I glanced up, it felt like half the campus was staring—like they'd heard me say it out loud. Did I really stick out that much? How small is this campus really anyway?

I kept munching on the bread and had a few handfuls of the sugar cake popcorn. In between the crunches I could hear a group of passerbys and it's not like I can turn my ears off. One of the three girls asked, "Did they ever find him? What was his name?"

"Garrett. And I don't know, he probably just withdrew or something," the second replied.

"Yeah, but like, what about his car?"

Then they were gone.

Garrett? Who's Garrett? *Find him?*

I tried not to dwell on it. Instead, I let Sylvia creep

back into my mind, her name slinking through the cracks like a trespasser. I closed my eyes and surrendered, just for a second. I pictured her sun-kissed skin, the photo where her heartbeat looked like it was trying to claw its way out of her chest based on her blushed cheeks and crows feet as she smiled.

I tried to think I was just being crazy thinking people were staring until a pudgy brunette mouth breathing girl walked over to me with pursed lips. She smiled, a little too wide and practiced for comfort, "You Edith?"

"Who's asking?" I said, eyeing her like a stray dog. Wary of teeth.

"Penelope Pendleton." Her voice was too smooth, like she'd rehearsed it in the mirror until it fit.

I raised an eyebrow. *Penelope Pendleton.* If ever a name came with a trust fund and a knife behind its back, it was that one.

She tightened her smile—stretched thin like overused elastic. "Syl told me you'd be around."

"Great. And you are…?"

She rolled her eyes, already bored. "Does it matter? Come on. I'll let you in." She turned and walked off without waiting.

I hesitated. I didn't know her. Didn't trust her. But my feet moved anyway, like they belonged to her.

"Are you leading me to my death or a side quest?" I called, jogging to keep up.

"Would a *friend* do either?" she tossed over her shoulder.

"You're not my friend," I shot back, sharper than I meant to.

"Ah, but Syl is," she said, glancing back. "Which means I *have* to be." She muttered it like a curse.

I pretended not to hear. I couldn't screw this up—not before I'd even started.

We walked through a wrought-iron gate and up a tree-lined path. The air felt wrong—too still. That kind of quiet that sits heavy on your ribs. Penelope filled it with small talk.

"So. How do you know Sylvia? I've barely heard anything about you, except that you were coming."

"Childhood friends," I said flatly. Just enough to satisfy her.

"Friends by proximity. Love that," she said, sarcasm sharp as glass.

I didn't answer. My skin prickled, that feeling you get when someone's staring too long. I glanced back. Nothing. Just empty shadows pooling under the trees. Still, the feeling stayed, sticky and unwelcome.

As we reached the front porch, it felt like the world stood still. Penelope bounced inside, but I hesitated at the door. The leaves stopped rustling, the wind halted. A faint ringing in my ears filled the lack of sounds. My first impression was that it was a beautiful place, but I wasn't even inside and it was giving me the creeps. It was too perfect, almost like someone had curated it just for me. Light filtered through the windows just so. Like a photograph come to life.

I stepped inside. Half-expected a ghost or a spider to greet me, but it was just the squeak of floorboards underfoot. Something in the air—vinegar and burnt paper—made me sneeze. The walls were faded white, paint peeling in curled strips. I shut the warped door behind me. Looked up. The crown molding—damn—was carved, hand-done, intricate.

To the left, a massive bay window spilled golden light across the floor. *This* was where I could live. Curled under a blanket with a book, tucked into that window like it was made for me.

Penelope's voice snapped me out of it. She hung her coat with flair. "I'm sure you've heard plenty about me and Syl's wild times. She's like a sister, you know?" She placed a hand over her heart, but her eyes darted to mine, searching for a reaction.

I gave a lazy shrug, trying to play it cool. "Yeah, she mentioned something about that."

Penelope's lips curled in a way that suggested she found the notion ridiculous, "No she didn't! You haven't talked to her in years." She opened her mouth like she was going to go further and quickly shut it, clearly holding back.

Something white-hot sparked in my eyes. My ears roared. I barely registered her yammering about her family's soy business.

"...so, have you?" she asked.

"Have I what?" I said, dazed.

"Pendleton Farms?" she said, a little sharper.

"I—what? No," I mumbled.

"Forget it." She turned toward the stairs, leaving me in the thick, muffled quiet. It felt like wearing noise-canceling headphones—no echo, no depth. Just pressure.

I gripped the banister and followed. She led me to a small room above the front door. It barely fit a desk, nightstand, and twin bed.

"A bit small," Penelope piped, "but it has the necessities, a closet and a *view*!" She presented the beautiful display of marble slabs and trees as if it was an oceanfront view in Miami.

The room was quaint, and I also loved the view. The city's buzz juxtaposed with the cemetery's stillness felt surreal. Penelope hovered too close, and a chill crept up my spine. I took a nervous inhale and smelled something odd. Is there a candle lit? Paper burning? I wrote it off and zoned in on whatever Penelope was droning about. Her voice was shrill, sending a searing pain to my eardrums, "Neat, huh? It's old as shit, and there's probably like a million ghosts roaming around, but the view's nice."

"Sublime," I murmured, still staring out at the cemetery.

"Welcome to The Flats." I glanced over and caught a thin-lipped of her cryptic smile before she shut the door behind her.

I stood there, dazed. I'd made it. I was in. But the weight of it didn't feel like triumph.

It felt like Sylvia.

I collapsed onto the bed. The mattress sank. The frame creaked, almost snapped.

Penelope was right. It had been years. I wasn't the same. She couldn't be either.

Chapter Three

Before

There was never a time I didn't want to be around Syl. In a town as small as ours, it was obvious she was top-tier—maybe not technically the most popular girl in school, but damn close. We didn't get into much trouble as kids, but when you're always orbiting the same person, trouble becomes inevitable.

When we were nine, we took her dad's golf cart and tore across acres of backwoods and farmland. We launched over hills, crashed through brush, grinning like lunatics. It felt endless, like we'd ride that thing forever—until the gas ran out and we pushed it home, still laughing.

I still remember our first fight. One day in late autumn the grass had all dried out and the leaves dead on the ground. We would do donuts all around the field without having a care about leaving tracks in the grass. Since she was driving she insisted I feed her a bag of chips. So I did.

She kept going in donuts while I had no grip. I begged her to stop, "No! Syl, no, don't do it!"

"Fine! Such a baby. Feed me another chip," she implored with

a snap of her fingers.

So I did.

I was met with another fierce drift and I flew off the side. Rolling and tumbling, the bag of chips still in my grasp.

There was no moving after a shock like being flung off the side of a moving vehicle, so I just laid there until she stopped laughing. Hoping she thought I was dead and she would be in big trouble.

I couldn't play dead for long because she grabbed me so hard I thought it would bruise and shook me for dear life, "Edie! Wake up! Are you alive!?"

When she saw the smirk breaking through my face, she slapped my arm.

"You scared me! I thought I killed you."

"It hurt," I snapped. "I told you to stop."

"Yeah, well I thought you were kidding. You should've said it for real."

Then she crossed her arms. "Stop being mad or I won't be your best friend anymore."

And that was that. I shut up. Because she was it—my whole world. No other friends mattered. Not then, not through high school. I realized that day what it would mean to lose her. I didn't just want her. I needed her—and I needed her to need me too.

Later, she gave me fifty bucks, a bag of Cheetos, and a Cosmic Brownie as a peace offering. It felt fair at the time.

We grew. A few inches, a few years. But the pattern stuck. It became my joy—and my curse—to give her everything she asked for. Whether I agreed or not didn't matter. When she said she'd stop being my friend, I'd cry myself to sleep. The nightmares of her leaving—of being abandoned like my dad left—would haunt me for weeks.

But it wasn't all bad. We had a rhythm. I did something for her, she'd do something for me. Always even. Always balanced.

Like the night after I got my license. A guy I only dated through text wouldn't walk with me in the hallway to class. She took my phone that night and texted him the cruelest break up message and insisted we go to the store to get brownie stuff. Her parents weren't strict, but she wasn't allowed out after nine.

"Oh, come on, Mom," Syl begged, literally on her knees, head in her mom's lap. "It's just to the store and back."

Her mom sighed. "Alright. But make it quick."

We bought two dozen eggs. Used half of them to egg the guy's house.

It was the most fun I'd ever had. Something about doing the wrong thing—for the right reason—was electric. I threw eggs at the mailbox like it owed me money. Syl suggested we park down the road to get his car.

"It'll screw up the paint," she grinned.

"That's too far," I said. "Isn't it?"

She looked at me—really looked. That fierce, focused stare. My body answered before I could.

"Alright," I whispered.

We parked a quarter mile away, thinking we were untouchable—until red and blue lights flared behind us. Busted.

Luckily, Syl's dad knew the sheriff. We got off with a warning. The boy's family didn't press charges. But I still got the dreaded line: We'll call your mom in the morning to inform her what you've done.

They sent me to Syl's room while she stayed downstairs for a "family meeting."

Of course I sat at the top of the stairs.

Her mom spoke first. "Syl, I know you love spending time with your friend, but I think this is getting out of hand."

"Mom, she's my best friend. We're just being teenagers. And

he deserved it."

Her dad chimed in, "Darlin', it's late. Can't this wait till morning?"

"No, Bill. This needs to happen now." Her mom sighed. "We need to talk about Edith. I know she's been your best friend since you two were in diapers, but... I think she's a little—how do I put it—eccentric—"

"Stop chomping your cheek and spit it out," her father said, tired and annoyed.

There was another sigh, and then: "We don't think you should be spending so much time with her. Because—well—"

He finished it for her. "Because we think she's a lesbian, honey."

Lesbian. The word hit me like ice water.

I sat against the banister. Frozen. I'm not able to sleepover with Syl anymore? We've done this our whole lives, what have I fucking done to them? Besides, it was Syl's fucking idea. It's not fair. Their accusation wasn't fair. They think it's alright to throw around "Lesbian"? Their words began to gnaw at me, and splinter under my skin. I hated them for saying it. And I hated that some part of me knew they were right.

Chapter Four

I heard her calling my name as I drifted in and out of consciousness. Her voice was warm, buttery—sliding straight down my spine like melted sugar.

"Edith…"

She was already in my dreams, teasing me and making me blush. Syl's grip had always been firm and greedy, but now she was so close I could feel her breath. Our souls were on the brink of aligning just before she kissed me. I woke breathless, moaning her name.

"Syl…"

"Edith." Her voice was just like my dream. She grabbed my arm so hard I could feel the bruise forming, shaking me, "Are you alright? Wake up!"

I groaned. "What time is it?"

"Nine. Why?"

I rubbed my eyes, still groggy, still unsure. But there she was.

Syl stood in front of me, impossibly real. Her chestnut-blonde hair hung in soft waves, smelling like rain and lemon. Her blue eyes met mine, electric and searching. Even more beautiful than the photos.

"What?" she asked, eyebrows knitting. "Why are you looking at me like that?"

"How long were you in class?" I sat up, pushing the blanket aside.

She lifted her shoulders. "It ended at four, but then I had two back-to-back. Penelope told me she found you exploring in the square. What do you think?"

"S'good."

"I'll give you a real tour tomorrow. Come on, you have to meet everyone." Syl hopped up from the floor and headed for the door.

I muttered, "Everyone? How many are there?" I'm already dreading the forced niceties.

"Well, you already met Penelope. She's a bit dry, but she's great. Don't mind Emberly if she's quiet. And Harriet—she's the sweetest and wicked smart, a pre-med." Syl grabbed my hand. A familiar spark flared up the second she touched me. "See? Not so bad! Come on."

She turned back and pulled me into a hug, laughing softly. "I'm so glad you're here. It's been too long." She kissed my cheek, her lips cool against my flushed skin. I went pink. My heart skittered.

"You sure you're okay?" she asked, her tone shifting as she brushed the hair from my face and laid the back of her hand against my forehead. "You're burning up."

"I'm fine," I lied, voice shaky. My brain was still spinning. Syl was here. Touching me. Acting like it was nothing. She didn't notice how wrecked I felt. She kept hold of my hand as we descended the stairs.

The floor creaked beneath us. The silence below was heavy—expectant. At the dining room threshold, it felt like I was walking onstage.

"Everyone, this is Edith, my greatest friend." Syl gave me a gentle push forward. "Edith, meet Harriet Wentworth and Emberly Stratton. You know Penelope already."

"Pleasure to meet y'all," I said, my voice too steady. I swiped a finger under my eye, trying to look composed.

Penelope looked like she smelled something foul.

Harriet offered a mild hum and a tight smile. Her platinum hair and strange galaxy eyes made her look ethereal—unsettling. She sat statuesque, as though she moved only when necessary.

Emberly, on the other hand, gave me a slow once-over, "Pleasure."

Her tone oozed with something unspoken as her lips curled into a smile that could pass for disdain. Emberly's gaze lingered on my chest for a second too long, and a rush of heat washed over my body involuntarily. I could feel my nipples tightening under her stare.

Our eyes met again, and she gave a full-toothed smile this time. Emberly knew the effect she had on women like me. I should have been embarrassed by her mentally undressing me, but I wasn't. Quite the opposite.

Syl interjected, her voice light but edged. "Em, don't play with your food. She might go back into her shell!" Syl shot me a mischievous grin, then added, "Even though I know it's cracked." She looked me dead in the eyes as she confessed, "Your mom wrote to me. Told me you're writing a thesis on *smut*, so you can't possibly be as shy as you used to be."

My stomach dropped. *Mother said what?*

Before I could react, Penelope cut in, tone acid. "People who read smut are pathetic. It's all so unrealistic."

Emberly leaned back, amused. "Afraid of a PQ, Pen?"

"PQ?" Harriet murmured, still staring into the table.

"Don't worry about it, Harry," Penelope snapped. "At least I don't waste my time on fake stories and PQs. I live the real thing."

The room shifted. Not in a big, obvious way—but enough. Harriet flinched like she'd been hit.

Syl laughed. Emberly rolled her eyes. "That's not how it works, Pen."

Penelope's face was taut, color high in her cheeks. No one else said a word.

I hovered in the silence, not sure if I was supposed to laugh, defend Harriet, or just pretend I didn't see anything. My stomach twisted then growled audibly. Syl slung an arm around my shoulder.

"We're off," she announced, tugging me toward the kitchen.

"Where?" Penelope called after us.

"Nunya. Edith, let's go."

Syl grinned, grabbed my hips, and steered me out the back door. I glanced back to see Penelope's face souring as we left.

Outside, the boards beneath our feet creaked. Below the deck, something flickered. A screen door framed a pale blue wooden door—padlocked.

"What's that?" I asked, halting.

Syl barely looked. "Used to be an apartment in the '50s. Now it's just a maintenance basement. Don't really know what's down there."

She kept walking, but something planted me in place, entranced by the fixture. I heard her call out, "Come *on*! Let's get out of here before twat face decides to tag along."

I offered, "She could have come," but didn't mean it.

"Don't worry about Penelope," she said, backing the car out of its space. "She can't *stand* feeling left out."

"I wanted you to myself tonight," Syl admitted with a wink as she turned on the radio.

I felt my heart skip, a fire kindling in my chest.

"Where are we going?" I asked, trying to focus on something else.

"You like dim sum, right?"

"Fuck yes."

She placed a hand on my knee, her stare piercing.

"I know a place with the best."

The engine roared. I rolled down the window, let the cold air hit my face.

"Take me away," I said.

Chapter Five

We'd called ahead and parked under a tree, the car tucked into the shadows, hidden from the world.

"Takeout or dine-in?" Syl asked.

I gave her a look. "You can probably guess."

She smirked, tilting her chin like she had the world in her back pocket, then slipped out to grab our order.

I stayed put, nestling deeper into my seat.

When she came back, the car filled with the rich, intoxicating scent of pulled pork buns and fried chicken dumplings. Who needed a table when you could eat in the dark and people-watch in peace?

She handed me chopsticks and Styrofoam containers dripping in dark soy sauce and chili oil. I was already salivating.

We went for the dumplings first. They burned, but the pain was addictive—chewy dough, greasy meat, the fat coating our lips. It was perfect.

I tried to stay focused on the food, but my eyes kept drifting. Syl licked each finger slowly, one by one. The soft sucking sound made my stomach twist.

Get a grip.

She was hotter than the damn chili oil.

The thought of past sleepovers made my skin prickle with heat. One touch from her right now, and I'd combust.

I forced my attention back to the food, distracting myself. But my mind couldn't stop flipping between whether I wanted to be her or fuck her.

She'd always had this hold on me. Even when she wasn't around, I couldn't get her out of my system. It had been two years, but one look, one touch, and I was done for.

A car passed by, headlights sweeping over us. That's when I saw Syl biting her bottom lip, her gaze distant but still locked on me.

Fuck.

We finished the food, licking the sauce from the bottom like animals. After that, the conversation softened—casual updates, safe topics. But the real conversation stayed buried between us, unspoken and heavy. Like a passenger neither of us invited.

I kept talking, pretending I'd done more than I had. Told her I was too busy to text, too deep in my work. Truth was, I rarely left my room.

"I've really gotten to know myself the past two years," I said, leaning hard into the lie. "Been diving deep into my research."

The truth? I read too much romance, got lost in stories about love I'd never find. When that didn't cut it, I turned to porn—hours of it—closing my eyes just to finish because none of it looked like what I really wanted. What I *craved.* What I couldn't say.

Even on the drive over, I couldn't stop ogling her.

Every bump in the road made her chest bounce, the radio light tracing the tops of her breasts. I watched them jiggle in rhythm and hated how much I loved it.

Syl leaned across the console, her eyes wide and playful. "So... who is Edith now? Does she still want me?"

Her fingers brushed my arm.

Her question sent shockwaves through me. I turned to face her, forcing the words out. "You know me." And yet, she didn't realize that right now, the only thing I could think about was tearing off that plaid mini skirt with my teeth.

"Do I?" Her eyes were sharp and cutting through my false confidence. For a moment, it felt like she was sizing me up as prey waiting to be claimed.

I feared she could see me. *All* of me. I couldn't tell what she was thinking and it scared the shit out of me.

My breath caught. I looked at her delicate lips as she spoke, the softness of her voice pulling at me. "Yes," I managed.

"Good." And just like that, she leaned back. The moment passed. But the tension stayed, thrumming under my skin.

I turned away, heart pounding, ashamed of how easily I folded. I'd barely been here for a day, and already she had me unraveling. My emotions were a wreck—love, lust, shame, confusion—blurring into one.

Whiplash.

Syl wiped her fingers, then stepped out to toss the trash. I watched her walk, every step illuminated by the moonlight, the shadows clinging to her in just the right ways.

I wasn't afraid of wanting her. I was afraid of what might happen if I reached for her.

The car door swung open, snapping me out of it.

She wore a wild grin. "Okay, so I gotta tell you something…"

I braced. "What?"

She reached into her jacket pocket and pulled out a cone joint. "Old times, right? You still smoke?"

As she rummaged for a lighter, I watched her face, her fingers.

"Uh, yeah. You still hotbox?"

She answered by settling back in her seat and rolling up the window.

***

Syl kept driving as we passed Cemetery Road, into the historic district. The houses grew scarce, trees closing in like curtains. Darkness swallowed us whole.

Syl flicked off the headlights and rolled into a vacant lot tucked behind a row of evergreens.

"Syl, what are we doing? The joint's almost out."

She didn't answer right away. Then, "We need complete privacy."

Syl cut the engine. The silence hit hard, pressing in around us until my ears started to ring. The tension becomes thinner with each passing second.

She put the joint's cherry in her cup holder ashtray and leaned across the middle console over me, her face inches from mine. Her fingers curled into my hair, tugging just enough to make me shiver. One hand gripped the back of my head while the other traced along my jaw, holding me in place. I was melting into the seat, but her touch anchored me there, steady and sure.

Everything about her felt balanced, deliberate, safe, even. Years of longing dissolved into the softness of her lips pressing against mine, a mutual understanding passing between us. I didn't know if it was the chili oil or the kiss making my lips burn, but I didn't care. All I knew was Sylvia fucking Harrington was kissing me, and it felt like both salvation and collapse.

When she pulled back, I was dazed. My lungs forgot how to breathe.

"Get in the back," she said, voice ragged.

My brain short-circuited. "Really?"

She didn't smile. Just grabbed my chin between her fingers, firm and deliberate.

"Do I need to ask again?" Her voice was warm and magnetic now. My desire for her was primal and overwhelming, but the personality switches were becoming cumbersome.

She was close, sending a ripple of goosebumps from head to toe. My body betraying me. Does she not see the effect she has on me? Hearing her say my name was nearly enough to undo me.

No.

I shouldn't do this, but I was already moving. I slid out of the car and into the backseat. Forcing myself not to rush, trying to appear calm when everything inside me was anything but. Years of craving this moment made my skin prickle, making it challenging to breathe evenly.

I sat next to her, heart pounding, chest tight. My breath comes in uneven gasps. I tried to steady myself, waiting for the magical moment I'd fantasized about.

But when I opened my eyes, she wasn't making any move to climb on top of me. She was grabbing another spliff and sparking the lighter.

Don't lose it.

I slunk down, draping my legs over the console, hiding my disappointment behind a curtain of hair. I wanted to scream. I wanted to *laugh* at myself.

Syl passed the joint to me. I took a long drag, letting the smoke ground me.

We were just two friends, getting high. Like before. Pretending nothing had happened. Pretending my insides weren't unraveling.

I exhaled. "Like old times. Right?"

She smiled, soft and distant. "They were great." She puffed. "Now look at us."

I stared at the glowing tip of the joint. "You surprised me—reaching out."

She didn't answer right away. Just leaned her head back against the seat.

"I needed time," she said at last. "Time to figure out who I was. Without the noise. Without anyone. That town…" She trailed off. "I couldn't breathe there."

I nodded, swallowing my disappointment. "It's okay. You don't owe me anything."

Still, I wanted her to say more.

She looked over, maybe sensing it. "Thanks," she said, and her voice, for once, was almost shy.

***

We smoked until we could taste the filter, and the

awkwardness between us seemed to lift. A milky fog filled the car. The steering wheel, the windows, every outline a blur.

I hadn't breathed this easily in years. My mind felt dazed but full of clarity in a way that only happens when you're high. Everything makes sense and loops back into nonsense.

"Oh my god, remember that P.E. teacher? What was his name? Mr. Spitting Gas?"

I rolled onto Syl's shoulder, choking on my laughter. "No! Mr. *Spatingas!*"

"Yeah, well, he was Spitting Gas after that fart in health class."

We lost it. Tears, wheezing, stomach cramps. We laughed until it hurt.

Then the high shifted. The air got heavier. Our breathing suddenly too loud, like we were both hyperaware of the closeness.

She leaned toward me, lips parted, and for a second I was sure this was it. She was going to kiss me. The tension was unbearable.

Then she said, softly, "You know, if things were different I…" From the outside, no one could make us out through the smoke fog. It didn't matter. The world outside didn't exist.

What was she about to tell me? "Come on, don't do that."

She leaned back and away from my proximity and the pang of disappointment struck me in the chest. Syl took a drag and shook her head, "I just miss my parents that's all. I don't know what I was saying, I have Discordia now.

And it doesn't matter, nothing would change."

Syl was making me greedy, and for the first time in years, I let myself be. I'd waited so long for a moment like this. I wasn't going to let it die in a puff of smoke.

Syl straddled my lap.

I stopped breathing.

Her hair flipped to one side as she leaned in, lips brushing my neck. Every part of me lit up. I wanted to sink my teeth into her skin, memorize every inch. When she bit the nape of my neck, I nearly lost it.

Her hips rocked forward, pressing into mine. I gasped.

Our fingers tangled in each other's hair, kisses sharp and hungry. Urgent. This was Syl—*mine now*. Or so I thought. The girl I used to watch from the corner of every room. The one I thought I'd never touch.

But now she felt different. Wilder. Raw. Like a new version of herself she hadn't shown anyone else.

I was spiraling.

"Edith?" she whispered against my lips.

"Yeah?" My voice cracked.

She pulled back slightly, her hands on my chest. "We should stop."

My stomach dropped. "Why?"

She sat back, shoulders tense, eyes not quite meeting mine. Her fingers traced the steering wheel like she was stalling.

"I understand."

"I knew you would," she said, finality in the words. But I didn't.

She hopped off my lap, the warmth of her body

leaving me cold. Her hands detached from my hips. The rejection was sharper than I expected. The sting of believing I'm wanted. It's never enough.

Emptiness slithered in and up my spine. Wrapping around my throat, choking me silently.

No amount of weed could convince me we couldn't make *something* work when I leave. She acted like the distance was cross-country, not a couple of hours. What was her game? Closure?

I didn't press for answers as we got back in the front seats. If she spoke to me, I wouldn't be able to respond. All I could do was appear indifferent as if she didn't tear my heart from my chest. Syl looked unbothered, which made me feel insane.

The air in the car felt colder, with things I'd left unsaid. I half-expected her to say something, but instead, she just turned toward the square. Her hand hovered above the gearshift a second too long. She didn't speak. Neither did I.

I should've stopped this earlier. Should've known better.

***

The walk across campus was tense, quiet. Shadows twisted up the brick and cobblestone, the trees clawing over the paths like something alive.

"You seem anxious," Syl said, cutting through the silence.

"Do I?" I tried to sound casual. I wasn't about to admit I was still reeling from her touch—or from the flickering lamps that lit up as we passed, one by one. I couldn't shake the feeling they were watching.

"We're just here for dessert," she said, brushing it off. "Then we'll go back to the flat."

Her tone was clipped. I didn't press. I didn't have the energy.

Inside the student center, it felt like we'd stepped into another timeline. Bright, modern and polished. It didn't belong here like someone had dropped a piece of the future in the middle of the past. I hated it.

A colossal machine at the back of the store was loud, and the students were boisterous, drowning out all thoughts. I swear I overheard multiple people say, "Missing." Over and over in different clusters. The repetitive S's catching my attention.

We grabbed ice cream cups and headed over to the whirring milkshake machine.

"Is something missing?" I said, raising my voice to be heard over the sound.

Syl leaned in closer to ask me, "What do you mean?"

Something in her pointed tone made me pause. "I feel like everyone keeps saying something is missing…"

She glanced at me, her eyes catching mine for a split second before looking away and looking at everyone. "I mean, yeah, some*one*."

"What?! Who?!" my curiosity spiked.

"He was just a day student here that went missing recently. No biggie."

"No biggie? Come on, there could be a psycho killer on this campus right now! What if he's lurking in the brush somewhere? It's not like it's well lit here and I haven't even seen a security officer here not once!"

"It's always about the men. If a woman did it, no one would even notice. She'd be hiding in plain sight."

I blinked. "You think a *woman* made him disappear?"

She smiled, zipped her lips with two fingers, then gave a shrug.

"No one ever suspects what the women are up to."

"You're insane." I laughed nervously. "Isn't that a little extreme for a place like Discordia?"

Syl raised a brow. "You can be small and still have secrets. The disbelief proves the point. Women here get what they want. And it's all thanks to *her*."

Her?

She turned back toward the snack shelves like she hadn't said anything unusual.

"I'd pity any man who tried something here. The pagans would have him sacrificed before dawn. The acolytes, too."

"Is this a school or a cult?" I asked, half-joking.

From somewhere in the distance, church bells began to chime. I looked at the clock behind us near the grille and saw that it was thirty-seven after. "And what is with that damn bell! It's been wrong every time I've heard it."

Syl just laughed, "Oh, it's always like that. That's Discordia for you." I could have sworn I distinctly heard something darker in her tone. "Don't be so thick though. This place opened a new world for me. They can do the same for you. I mean, once I came here and got initiated I've never looked back and I don't want to. This place and the people in it, it's all I need."

"I'm only here for a week," I replied, trying to keep my voice light.

There was an edge to Syl's response I couldn't ignore as she said, "For now."

A loud rattling from the machine made us both jump and it made the nape of my neck itch excessively. The sound was as if the machine was about to explode. A cook emerged, rolling his eyes, and slapped a sign on the machine: "Out of Order."

The crowd groaned in chorus.

Outside again, Syl's voice was softer. "My first week here, I realized I'd been asleep. Coming here woke me up."

Maybe she was right. Maybe I'd been asleep too. A small, quiet bloom of power stirred in my chest.

"Let's hit Cookout," she said suddenly. "They've got the best milkshakes."

"It's 1 a.m."

"They're open. Come on."

I didn't argue. "I'm with you."

We walked past the square. She held out an arm to stop me.

"Speak of the little devils."

A circle of girls sat in the grass, eyes closed, hands raised. A ritual.

"What the hell are they doing?" I whispered.

"Their weekly séance," she said. "Probably hexing their exes or doing love jars. Nothing serious."

Too freaky. I looked away. "Right."

She didn't laugh. As we walked back to the car, I felt lighter—and heavier. Syl hadn't gone full witch. That was... something.

Still, unease crept back in. The cobblestones cracked under our steps. Wind hissed through the trees, scattering leaves like warnings.

Her words echoed in my head: *It's all thanks to her.*

Who?

I glanced at Syl. She looked ahead, confident, untouchable.

I didn't know if she wanted me or just wanted control. But I knew one thing: time wasn't on my side. And whatever I thought this trip would be—it was already becoming something else entirely.

For now, I would have to settle for the time I had.

***

We left the dim streets behind and entered the glare of the city. After a few quick turns, the massive Cookout sign came into view—red neon spinning in the night, cutting through the white fluorescents.

I'd heard of Cookout. Never seen one in person. Never at one in the middle of the night.

"Why are there so many people here?" I asked, eyeing the snaking drive-thru line, headlights catching every dusty curve of the car.

"For the same reason we are," Syl said smoothly.

We crawled forward, car by car. Time stretched thin between each stop.

At the intercom, she asked, "What milkshake do you want?"

I stared at the menu. Too many choices. My brain blurred the options into a slurry of sugar.

"Uh… Oreo?"

Syl leaned in, voice syrupy with mischief. "You sure, Edith?"

The way she said my name came out thick with her tongue peeking out of her supple lips. She knew precisely what she was doing, pulling me deeper into a trance with every syllable.

I straightened up, embarrassed by how obvious my reaction must have been. "Caramel Oreo, please," I said, trying to regain some control over myself.

We finished ordering and inched forward, watching the cars ahead get their orders one by one at a snail's pace. The consistent thrumming of the car's engine should have grounded me but I couldn't take it anymore, "Okay, I have to know. If this isn't a cult, then what is this initiation thing really about?"

Her smirk was slow, knowing. "Well, if you *must* know—freshman initiation happens at dawn, in the amphitheater. All the girls wear white. We sing devotionals to the goddess Discordia. We carry beeswax candles…"

"Wait—candles? White gowns?"

She nodded, eyes distant, a soft glow behind her words. "It's beautiful. We light each other's candles, singing in unison. It binds us—to each other, to her."

"Her?"

"Discordia. Then we walk up to the cemetery. Everyone brings a trinket, something personal. We leave it on the founder's grave as an offering."

I waited. "And?"

"And some come back the next morning to see what's been taken."

"Taken? You mean by Discordia herself?"

She didn't laugh. "If she's pleased, the offering's gone. If it's still there… well, that says something."

"Couldn't someone just clean it up? A groundskeeper or—?"

"No." Syl snapped toward me, her lips thin as a razor, "No. It's real. We don't disobey the tradition here. It's for *her*."

"But how do you *know*?" I skepticized.

"Well, there was one time I did it last semester. I offered something *very* personal. No one knew I had went, and the next day, it was gone before sunrise. So I don't know Edith, I just know."

I would never forget her like this. So changed, yet that brashness I recalled seemed to remain. She had this way of spinning control and spontaneity into something powerful, something I craved even though I knew I shouldn't. The neon lights outside bathed Syl in an eerie glow that made her into a sultry, blood-filled vision. She emanated love and passion, but something else undoubtedly sinister lurked beneath.

I didn't care. I couldn't stop gushing over her despite my better judgment. Whatever she was. Good, bad, in between. It didn't matter, I was undeniably hers. This limbo she kept me in, it was unbearable. She never told me what she wanted. Never let me go either. I reached out, hesitated, then took her hand.

She turned to me, eyes gleaming with something sharp. I couldn't tell what she was going to do next. But then, just like that, she pulled away.

We reached the window. Our milkshakes exchanged hands. When her fingers brushed mine, I felt a shock of heat. I latched on, almost knocking the lid loose.

"What did you mean," I asked, "when you said, 'if

things were different'?"

The look on her face told me everything—and nothing. She had me. I knew it. She knew it.

"Then… maybe…" she teased, letting it hang.

My breath caught. I softened my grip, but didn't let go. I brought her hand to my lips. Just a brush, testing the limits. Her fingers didn't flinch. I kissed her again, slow and deliberate.

"Forgive me," I whispered. "But it's never been different for me."

I searched for any sign of what was on her mind. But still, there was nothing. She just stared through me, her face completely impassive. Diverting her eyes, she moved forward in the line. As she looked away, I noticed her pulse quicken in her neck, a tiny flutter that gave her away. That's when the car behind us honked, signaling we were holding up the line.

When her eyes left mine, I conceded to take whatever she offered me, even if it meant being left in the dark.

Chapter Six

The warmth of the house wrapped around me like a soft embrace as we stepped back into the Flats. Harriet stood in the kitchen, her back turned, placing a kettle on the stove.

"Smells good," I offered, desperate to break the silence.

Harriet turned slowly, stiff and measured, like a machine learning to move. "It's water."

"Oh." I let out a nervous laugh—short, shallow. She mimicked me, beat for beat, until my laughter died in my throat.

"It's alright," she said flatly. Her voice returned to monotone.

Something in her gaze made me hesitate as she asked, "Tea?"

I wasn't sure if that was such a good idea. Her eyes locked onto mine, holding a second too long. The silence stretched, her gaze feeling like a challenge.

"Sure," I said, even though I wasn't entirely sure what she was making.

"Sylvia?" she asked.

"None for me," Syl replied, casually leaning down to peck Harriet on the head. "You make nothing less than perfect every night, Harri."

Harriet's thin lips twitched, the faintest hint of a smile that gave me the creeps. So I trailed behind Syl down the hallway. She turned, putting her hands up to stop me, "I'll be back. Edith, why don't you stay for tea?" she said, already halfway down the hall. "I'll be back."

I watched her disappear upstairs, leaving me alone with Harriet, whose presence felt suddenly enormous.

Syl's voice floated down, chipper and distant: "Want fuzzy socks? They pair great with Harri's tea!"

Relieved, I bolted up the stairs two at a time. Her door was open. She was face-down in her dresser, ass high, plaid skirt riding up her thighs. My brain betrayed me instantly with a flash of fantasy I tried to shove back down.

Get over yourself, Edith.

She emerged holding matching mocha-colored fuzzy socks, lace-frilled and impossibly cute. She handed them to me with a smile.

"I'm so glad you're here," she said softly as she hugged me, her breasts squishing into mine.

"Me too." My voice sounded tiny, hesitant.

Her hands rubbed my back a moment before she pulled back, squeezing my arms, "See you in the morning?"

"Right."

With a soft nod, Syl slipped into her room, "Goodnight." She said before closing the door with a faint click behind her. I stood there, feeling that familiar pull—wanting more but knowing better than to push.

I licked my lips, tasting the faint trace of Syl's chapstick still lingering there.

In your dreams, Edith. Let it go.

With a deep breath, I commanded my body and mind to calm down, steeling myself against the ache now settling into my chest. I counted back from three and headed into my room. Coat off. Shoes kicked aside. My favorite pajama set—the one with *The Stranger* printed all over, a gift from my mother—gave me a strange comfort. With my fuzzy socks already on, I brought my feet up to my nose and inhaled deeply, savoring the sweet smell of Syl's laundry detergent to give me strength. I heard the faint whistle of the kettle from downstairs and knew I couldn't avoid being social since I already agreed to have tea. It's time *to be social.*

I returned to find Harriet pouring hot water into a glass pot. Her movements were slow, precise, like she was handling glass already broken. I followed her into the living room, where I took the chair that wasn't surrounded by a chaos of science textbooks. The room was dim, every corner shadowed by flickering candlelight. The air was thick, like something unseen was watching.

Harriet returned with a tea setup fit for royalty— delicate china, ornate sugar bowls, even a tiny bread plate. It felt ceremonial. Too much for a midnight chat.

She moved with studied grace, placing each piece with surgical accuracy. It felt like I'd stumbled into a ritual halfway through.

"Fancy," I said, trying not to sound unnerved.

"That's why I stole them," she remarked, almost an afterthought, as she poured the tea, plopping two sugar cubes into her cup.

I blinked. "Wait, what?"

The corners of her lips twitched, barely noticeable. "Only joking. They were a birthday gift."

"You had me for a second," I admitted, rubbing the back of my neck.

Harriet hummed in response, sipping her tea with that same eerie calm. I lifted my cup to my lips. The first sip was heavenly and aromatic.

"This is amazing. Is it lavender?" I asked, holding my cup out as Harriet refilled it without a word.

"No," she replied, setting the pot down. "It's a blend I call 'Hawaiian Lotus.'"

"What's that?" I couldn't stop myself from drinking more. The taste was almost addictive.

"Hawaiian Baby Woodrose mixed with Blue Lotus. Took months to perfect. It opens the ethereal plane."

I froze mid-sip. "...The ethereal plane? Like... metaphorically?"

She leaned forward, voice hushed. "No metaphor. It's real. Tea is chemistry, Edith. Boiling water, precise ratios—unlocking the universe one step at a time. The key is to observe without ego and bias."

My stomach flipped, the warmth from the tea turning sour in my gut. "It's... delicious."

Even though it was delicious and made to perfection, her spiritual approach to making tea was frightening. Was this supposed to impress me? Or unsettle me? I wasn't sure, but I drank anyway, my body still buzzing with unease. Couldn't be any more of a sedative than Valerian root.

"It should be," she said, lips quivering in that eerie almost-smile. "They're hallucinogenic."

My heart slammed against my ribs, picking up pace, "Wait... what?"

Harriet's expression remained perfectly still, her voice unsettlingly tranquil. "I thought I mentioned it." She sipped her tea, a sliver of a smile curling at the edge of her lips.

Shit. As my mind processed what had happened, my stomach became weak, and I wanted to vomit all over the faded red patterned rug.

"If you fear the experience," she said, "sleep. Otherwise, it will be... prolonged."

I set the cup down, hands shaking. "I... I think I'll go to bed."

Harriet bowed slightly, serene. "Goodnight."

I stood, legs unsteady, skin clammy. Her eyes followed me like a painting in a haunted house.

I climbed the stairs, slower now. My limbs felt too heavy. I couldn't tell if I was already hallucinating or just panicking.

In my room, I locked the door behind me. I paced in organic shape formations while wiping sweat from my face and gathering my thoughts. There was no way I could throw up and make it go away. I already *drank two cups*! Plus, it's not like a pill. And what the fuck were those ingredients again? My memory was shit now, and I didn't even know what effects were about to take away all of my inhibitions. There was no choice but to do as Harriet instructed and sleep.

I lay on top of the comforter, the hot flashes refusing

to cease. Invisible bugs crawled over my skin, and it took physical effort to stop scratching. When I couldn't pull my hair from my head, I started gnawing on my fingernails. My mind begged for sleep, but my body refused.

***

I wake with a start, my eyes wide and my heart pounding. The room's edges are blurred, soft and wavering like a dream I can't shake. Shower. I need a shower.

Stealthily, I tiptoe through the hall, careful not to creak the floorboards as I reach the bathroom. The cold tiles ground me for a moment. I shut the door, flick on the yellow overhead light, and catch a glimpse of myself in the mirror—flushed and disheveled.

I strip quickly, desperate for the hot water. Steam fills the room almost instantly as I turn the faucet. I step under the scalding water, letting it cascade over me, burning my flesh. I chew on my cheek, forcing the thought away as I scrub my scalp. The water is practically boiling, but my body doesn't register it. It's something real I can cling to.

I rub the water from my eyes, looking for the shower caddy I forgot. "Shit."

I glance around the shower, unsure which bottle belongs to Syl. Would she mind? My pulse quickens at the thought of using someone's stuff without permission.

A knock on the door makes me jump.

I freeze, goosebumps rising as I hop out and quickly wrap a towel around myself.

The door creaks open, and Emberly's silhouette appears. My heart skips.

"What's up?" I ask, my voice shaky.

"I needed my toothbrush," she says, stepping inside, her eyes on me. "What are you doing?"

"I, uh... forgot my shower caddy."

"I can grab it for you."

I hold up both hands to decline, and my towel slips just below my breasts before I can catch it. I fumble and answer, "No, that's okay."

Emberly's gaze lingers, tracing the lines of my collarbones and dipping to where my hands clutch the towel.

"Do you want to use mine?"

I hesitate. "D'you mind?"

She steps closer, pointing out her shampoo and body wash.

"It's those."

I nod, unable to speak. Emberly leans in, her breath warm against my ear.

"I like the idea of you wearing my scent," she whispers, then slips out of the bathroom before I can respond.

Careful, Edith.

***

When I finally return to my room, I feel like raw meat— exhausted and tense. I collapse into bed, pull on my boy shorts and an oversized shirt. My body aches, but deep sleep never comes.

The night stretches endlessly as I slip in and out of consciousness. My eyes dart to the door, which creaks open slowly. I don't dare move—not that the weight on my chest would allow it.

A white raven perches on a chair by the threshold, its dark eyes piercing me. It flies to my chest, its beak and talons sharp, breaking skin.

I jolt awake, gasping for breath, heart racing. Relief washes over me as I move, flexing my limbs. I stand too quickly. The world spins. My legs give out, and I collapse to the floor with a thud.

***

"Edith, what the fuck?"

Syl's voice pulls me back. I blink, vision blurry, and realize she's cradling me. Sunlight spills into the room.

"Are you alright? What happened?"

"I'm fine," I mumble. "Stood up too fast."

"You scared the shit out of us," Syl says, helping me sit on the edge of the bed.

I glance up and see Emberly leaning in the doorway, her eyes veiled.

"I'll be fine," I say, the heat of embarrassment rising to my face. "I just need coffee. I'll be fine."

Syl glances at Emberly.

"Em, could you make her some?"

Emberly casts me a glance before heading downstairs. "Of course."

Syl stays a moment longer, her hand gently squeezing my shoulder.

"You sure you're okay?"

"Yeah. I'll take it slow," I answer, more curtly than I mean to.

Once Syl leaves, I let out a long exhale, needing a moment to collect myself. I close my eyes, the

45

embarrassment churning in my stomach before I swallow it.

When I open my eyes, the world steadies.

When I try to stand and regain my balance, I worry I've fucked everything up—any chance of fitting in. I only need to be myself, but this? This isn't like me at all.

Oh well, I think, *just a few more days.*

If anyone thought I was too much, they'd find less.

My attempts to soothe myself are futile because I desperately want to fit in.

Leave my old life behind for something like this.

I want to stay forever.

Chapter Seven

I braced myself. Standing before the mirror, I straightened my back, lowered my shoulders, and fixed any slight imperfections. A pair of eyes met my reflection—calm, unassuming, hiding what I felt beneath the surface. My face was a perfect mask.

Downstairs, voices buzzed—boisterous, filled with laughter. Each person a character, a distinct part of the group, but I couldn't see where I might fit. Would they accept me if I assimilated—or respect me more if I stood apart?

Taking my time descending the stairs, I listened as the wave of chatter grew louder. I spotted Emberly in the kitchen—focused, calm—pouring water from the gooseneck kettle in slow, deliberate circles.

I slipped into the kitchen before joining the others, my curiosity getting the better of me. Emberly worked with precision, the scent of fresh grounds filling the air.

"What's that?" I asked, unable to hide my interest.

"It's a roast from Charleston," she replied without breaking her rhythm. "I picked our best one for you. If you don't like it, toss it—I won't be offended."

I smiled. "It smells fucking amazing."

Emberly's lips quirked slightly before her usual solemn expression returned. The conversation ended, but I stayed, watching as she finished the pour-over. My patience wore thin as the smell hit me full force. My response was Pavlovian.

"Where are the mugs?" I asked, glancing around, unsure of which cabinet to search first.

Emberly set down the kettle without saying a word and handed me a mug. Our fingers brushed.

"Don't worry, Edie, I got you one."

"Thanks," I muttered, searching and hoping to find monkfruit sweetener. I found the half-and-half in the fridge but no sweetener.

"Sugar's on the island," Emberly said, still facing the coffee.

Great, no sweetener, then. I made a mental note to pick some up at a nearby store later. I wasn't a sugar fan, but it would do for now. I poured in the half-and-half and set the cup down next to the coffee pot, waiting.

Emberly caught me watching. "Do I look like I'm going to pour it for you?"

Caught off guard, I stammered, "I—"

"Relax," she said, a smirk tugging at the corner of her mouth. "I am."

I let out a breath. "Thanks."

As she poured the coffee, I inhaled deeply. The laughter and conversation in the dining room continued, but in the kitchen, it felt quieter—almost peaceful.

"Here you go," Emberly said, handing me the mug.

"Thanks," I replied, as if she did this for me daily.

We both headed to the dining room. When we entered, I was greeted by a bountiful spread—soft cheese samplings, sausage patties, toast, and a pot of soft-boiled eggs. Jams and butter lined the table, almost begging to be indulged.

Holy shit. It's like I'm in a Regency novel.

I glanced around, gesturing for Emberly to sit before I slid into the last open spot next to Syl. The conversation flowed around me, full of inside jokes, conspiracies, and philosophical debates. I tried to keep up.

Right now, they were talking about some professor who had shown up to a *Vagina Monologues* performance blackout drunk.

"She sat next to the Dean!" someone said, laughing.

"And didn't form a coherent sentence the entire night," another chimed in.

"She was on the floor the whole time. Fucking embarrassing."

Harriet, sitting at the head of the table, cut through the chatter. "It's time."

Realizing their cue, everyone quieted, bowing their heads as Harriet grabbed the beeswax candle from the candelabra and the others followed. So I did too. Harriet declared in an orans position,

"I burn for you, with you, as she would for me."

In unison, they raised their heads and began repeating the phrase together as they lit each other's candles. When it got to me, Emberly wouldn't light mine. They kept repeating the phrase. I noticed my body shrinking in the seat and quickly fixed my posture, reaching out with my candle toward hers. She retreated. I looked around, confused. The girls kept their eyes elsewhere. When Emberly finally looked at me again, I could hear her words—distinct from the others—urging me to join. So I begrudgingly did.

"I burn for you, with you, as she would for me."

Only then did she light my candle, allowing me to continue the circle. They repeated the phrase around ten times before it returned to Harriet.

The room fell silent, and I stopped as well. Harriet dropped her arms and said, "Remember what you stand for. What we stand for. Do not disappoint her."

Together they placed their sticks back in the candelabra and began serving themselves. As if on cue, a small breeze must have come through, because all the candles went out at once. Bewildered by the smoke rolling from the wicks, I thought someone might relight them—but no one did.

Why is that such a big deal?

I'll tell you when it would be a big deal: if this was a cult.

Reaching for my silverware, I tried to appear natural. I grabbed a slice of toast and cut it into neat strips. Reached for a soft-boiled egg from the pot, marvel at its farm-fresh bluish hue. The bacon was greasy as hell—a good in-between of crispy and chewy, but I'll pass. *Oh, that jam looks nice...*

I tried to make casual conversation.

"Finding eggs like this around here seems tough," I said. "How'd you get these?"

Harriet glanced up from her plate, a small, knowing smile tugging at her mouth.

"I know a farmer. He doesn't like eggs. I happen to love them."

"You barter?" I asked, raising a brow.

Harriet's smile deepened. "Something like that."

No one made a move to keep carrying the conversation as it drifted away again. I searched the table for the salt and pepper shakers.

After an eternity, I spotted them behind the pot, just out of reach. As I leaned forward to grab them, Emberly wordlessly handed them over.

"Thanks," I muttered.

Emberly nodded and returned to her local newspaper.

The shakers were beautiful—old-fashioned, silver, intricately carved with flowers and leaves. I shook the salt over my egg, but my eyes lingered on the bottom, trying to find the maker's stamp.

Ah. It's real!

Syl nudged me, prompting me to look down. I was mortified to see my egg buried under a mountain of seasoning.

"Shit. Sorry."

Pen looked over with genuine curiosity. "What's real?"

"The shakers. They're antique. I figured I might see them in a glass case in a permanent collection somewhere. Instead, they're accompanying my breakfast."

"Whoa. Harriet, why haven't you flipped them? I bet they're worth something! Those are yours, aren't they?"

"I can't appreciate them if they sit in a case somewhere. They're a family heirloom, sweet Pen. They're not for sale."

As their debate continued, Syl subtly handed me another egg from the pot.

The rest of the meal I tried to fade into the background. Penelope and Sylvia become giggly and animated, telling stories with wild gestures. Harriet and Emberly were quiet and observant, taking everything in without offering much of their own opinions.

Syl reached over, her hand resting on my knee.

"Did you get enough to eat?" she asked. "There's plenty left."

"I'm good, thanks," I replied.

"You sure? You seem... off."

Before I could answer, Penelope's nasal voice cut through the room.

"You don't have an eating disorder, do you?"

I blinked rapidly. "Would I be eating if I did?"

"Depends," she said with a shrug. Penelope looked like she was about to gauge my reaction, while the others looked wide-eyed and lost.

"Well, no," I said, a bit defensive.

Penelope smirked, launching into a story about a friend who had struggled with an eating disorder, spinning it into something that felt too personal and too careless for the setting. I noticed Emberly's eyes narrow at her.

"How do you figure Edith has an eating disorder? You just met her," Emberly asked, her voice sharp.

Penelope shrugged. "Well, she fainted yesterday, and all she's had today is coffee, toast, and one egg."

"That's a stretch, don't you think, Pen?" Syl said, a warning in her tone.

"As long as she feels sustained..." Harriet murmured, spearing a grape with her fork before changing the subject.

"What are you guys doing today?"

Penelope perked up as if waiting for her cue.

"I'm seeing a man. A real man."

Syl rolled her eyes. "I'm showing her around campus. We're stopping by the bakery."

I couldn't help but join in. "Their rosemary garlic bread is amazing."

Harriet nodded. "The aroma haunts me when I leave class in the main building. I have to physically resist every time."

Penelope waved her hand dismissively. "It's basic. The bakery downtown is much cheaper and just as good. Speaking of cheap, is no one going to ask about my date?"

"It's about the experience, Pen!" Syl said, animated. "That oven has been baking bread since the 1700s. A modern bakery downtown can't compare."

Penelope laughed. "It's not that deep, Syl!"

"It is that deep," Syl replied firmly. "This is about tradition. About living through history," she added, delivering her point with gusto.

Emberly peered up from her phone. "Is it a date, or are you spending forty minutes in his dorm and then hiding at the coffee shop for three hours to make it look like a date?"

Penelope glared. "Fuck you, Em. You know it's been hard to find anyone good since Garrett!"

Emberly smiled, showing all her teeth. A direct hit.

The room fell silent. There was that name again. I still didn't know who Garrett was, but I kept sipping my coffee, unwilling to break the tension crackling between them. I couldn't name it—this complex dynamic I had always been at the edge of in group settings. But it was fascinating to watch. So I waited, hoping someone else decided to break the silence.

To my dismay, we all finished breakfast, and no one said another word.

CHAPTER EIGHT

Before

When we were younger, Syl and I would snuggle through the night, limbs entangled as we drifted to sleep. Over time, our closeness never faded, but the meaning behind it began to change—at least for me. It wasn't until the night her parents told her I was a lesbian that my feelings crystallized into something far more profound, something I couldn't ignore any longer. Syl's beauty, inside and out, had transformed in my eyes. She defended me to no end, shouted at her parents they were wrong. Even though I didn't realize they were right, I found myself in love with her from across those same few inches. It wasn't like I just woke up and became gay. It was her mind and heart I fell in love with first. The way she was always there for me, the way my heart pounded when she was close to me, the way I felt white hot when she stared into my eyes. Our connection felt cosmic, and I was drifting in her orbit with no destination except closer and closer to her. It was close to the holidays and I had multiple scenarios where I could turn my Thanksgiving "I'm thankful for you" speech into something grande and spectacular to confess. If that didn't work I had an array of gifts that would definitely scream to the heavens

I'm in love with her as more than a friend.

But things changed when Syl got a boyfriend just before Thanksgiving.

She started coming around less, and I told myself it didn't matter. That we were still us. That our bond—sacred, unshakable—would withstand anything. But it did matter. It hurt. Did having a boyfriend mean she had to change? Did it erase what we had?

One night she came by. I reached to wrap my arms around her, like we always did when we had sleepovers, but she shifted away.

"We can't sleep like this anymore, Edie," she muttered, her back to me. Her voice landed like broken glass. "It's not appropriate. I have a boyfriend."

My voice caught. "But... you—"

"I'm straight, Edith," she said flatly, not even looking at me.

"Syl—"

She cut me off, turning just enough to shoot me a final glance. "Let's just go to bed."

After that night, Syl stopped coming by. Weeks turned into months, and summer crept in like a fog. I felt hollowed out, trying to adjust to the silence. She had been everything—my anchor, my constant.

And now the ground was gone beneath me. I felt pathetic. Lonely. Raw. Syl had been my foundation, and now I had to face the ache that left me half-awake most nights, staring at the ceiling.

When I couldn't take the distance any longer, I drove over around ten one night, hoping we could talk. Hoping we could find our way back to something.

Mr. Harrington answered the door, wheezing heavily, his mouth slack and breath thick with salt. He spit when he spoke.

"She ain't here."

"Her car's in the driveway. Look, Mr. Harrington, could I please just—"

He cut me off, stepping out and closing the door behind him. His bloated stomach bumped me back.

"Look, Edith," he said, voice low and grim. "I know you girls have been good friends, but I know what girls like you want, and I'm not letting you in past dinner time."

"But can't I just—"

He raised a hand inches from my face, silencing me.

"This isn't up for debate. Now run along. Maybe text her in the morning if you really want to talk. Go on now—I bet your mother's wondering where you are."

I stepped off the porch, seething, while he turned back inside and locked the door behind him.

I backed out of the driveway, but I didn't want to leave.

Something was wrong. I could feel it. And it was killing me to not know what.

Chapter Nine

The chipped paint fell in small flakes alongside the leaves swirling around us like snow as we shut the door. I heard the final, metallic *click* of the lock. Syl hadn't told me her plans—but what else was new? I'd follow her anywhere if it meant being alone with her.

We walked along the paved path beside the cemetery, acres of headstones stretching endlessly. The iron gates loomed ahead, groaning open as we approached, like they hadn't moved in years. Everything here felt heavier than the rest of the world. Modern life was designed to be light and efficient, but this place—sturdy, unyielding—seemed determined to outlast everything, no matter how worn it looked.

Thick gray clouds rolled overhead, making the colors of the houses and trees pop against the cobblestone streets. I'd only been here once before, but something about it felt oddly comforting. The cold wasn't crisp and dry—it seeped into my clothes, settled on my chest, and refused to leave. Red maple leaves skittered across the ground, and a chill crawled up my spine. Fall and winter in the South have this way of getting under your skin, into your bones.

Syl moved purposefully, veering left and guiding me down a narrow driveway beside an old church. The bell rang, marking the hour, but it felt like time had stopped for us.

"Where are we headed?" I asked, trying not to sound as unsure as I felt.

"You'll see," Syl said with a knowing smile like she always did when she had a secret she wasn't ready to share.

Of course I followed because what choice did I have?

We arrived at a building that looked like it had been stitched together by a dozen different hands—stone, glass, brick, even white siding all jumbled together in a strange temple to the arts. It shouldn't have worked, but somehow it did. Moss crept across the shingled roof, giving it a sense of age and quiet wildness.

"The Fine Arts Center," Syl announced, her voice almost reverent.

We walked a winding stone path around the building, past windows that gave glimpses into the art studio. Even during fall break, students were inside, palettes in hand. A still life sat at the room's center—fruit, candlesticks, and, oddly, a skull covered in lipstick kiss marks—unified by a massive swath of burgundy satin fabric.

Each student stood at an easel, eyes locked on their canvas like they were trying to unlock a secret. Then, all at once, they turned and looked at us. At *me*. Their eyes locked onto mine, and I froze. A prickling climbed the back of my neck. They knew we were there. We were intruding. Syl didn't seem to notice, or maybe she didn't care. The only movement was a couple students off to the left in a different area. One of the girls dragged the other across a large raw duck canvas the size of a rug. She kept moving, leading me onward, but I couldn't take my eyes off. When they stood up, I was shocked to see the remnants of what looked like a murder scene and the paint they used was the color of blood pools. Not the bright crimson red you might assume, but with brown mixed in with scarlet to make it more realistic. I only followed Syl to get a better look to make sure she wasn't hurt, "Is that even allowed?" I asked.

Syl came back to see what I was, "Oh. Yes, very unconventional. What, do you think the goddess would appreciate anything *but*?"

"Anything but death?"

"*Chaos*, Edie. How are we supposed to reach our full potential through conformity?" she scoffed.

"Who are you, and what have you done with Sylvia?"

She rolled her eyes and kept moving. "Come on. You need to see the exhibit."

As I looked back one last time, I forgot about the other students—their blank expressions still fixed on me until I slipped from view. I tugged the back of my shirt, sweat clinging to my skin, and followed Syl into the icy chill of the gallery. We reached a patio with six white doors lined like soldiers. Syl headed to the farthest one, scanned her student card, and the lock clicked open. We stepped inside.

The first thing I noticed was the choice in front of me: to the left, a long hallway stretched into the distance. Ahead, the vast gallery opened up. Syl was already moving toward the open space, but I lingered, watching her.

She moved like she floated. Her body's lines were graceful and fluid—it wasn't fair, how effortless it was for her. Not just moving through space. When Syl walked, it was like watching art in motion.

The gallery was bursting with vibrant color, every hue humming in the stillness. But none of it compared to Syl. She was the centerpiece. The masterpiece. Her presence was like a lullaby—or a jazzy French song. A soft, lilting melody that drew you in and suspended you.

I couldn't look away.

She flitted from piece to piece, barely looking at them. Supposed to be showing me around, she moved like she owned the space, like the art was background noise. It was borderline disrespectful—disregard for the artists, for the work. Meanwhile, I stood frozen, drinking her in.

Her laugh—soft and delicate, danced through the air, making everything feel lighter. She had no idea did she? I had no idea how much power she held, but it was crescendoing with each moment I spent with her. No idea the ripples she cast in the lake of my being just by existing.

I wish I could freeze this moment, make a painting of her. I honestly didn't care that she paid me no mind. I was lost thinking of how I could chisel out every inch of her from marble and remain the same forever. But I knew it wouldn't. The world would keep moving, even if I wanted it to stop.

Making a conscious effort to look away, I tried to stroll around and at least lazily appreciate the work. And I'm glad I did. An oddly lifelike sculpture caught my eye. A man, his face was contorted, somewhere between anguish and surrender. His posture suggested he was transitioning into a kneel, mouth open, tears streaming down his face. He could be wailing and close to putting his head in his hands, giving up entirely. The look of a man who knew he failed. I could feel it. The artist succeeded in making me feel torn between pitying him and laughing. Because what could a man have done to deserve feeling this way besides, in my humble opinion, being a victim to his own actions. I see the vision clearly and get the validation I was right when I see the label for the piece, *Regret*.

I continued down the corridor, admiring a post-impressionistic portrait series. All women, all dressed in white. Some danced, others posed traditionally in three-quarter frames. But the faces were different. Each had been carefully rendered, then erased—scrubbed with turpentine until only hints remained. Raw canvas, underpainting, nothing else.

The effect left me uneasy. The women hung on the wall to be admired—ogled—and suddenly I wasn't intrigued. I was off-put. Maybe that *was* the point.

After leaving the center, we strolled along the brick walkways into the heart of campus. The air felt sharper, more present. Birds sang in short bursts overhead, grounding me. The decaying leaves crunched under my Oxfords, life and death mixing beneath each step.

"I need to make a stop," Syl said, nodding to a small dorm that looked like a storybook cottage.

"I'm with you," I said.

As we got closer, I envied anyone who could live here. It was precisely like the cottages in illustrated children's books, with greenery scaling bottom to top, the brick busted on the brink of being condemned. It was definitely not what I expected a dorm to look like.

"Is this really a dorm? Looks like a two or three-bedroom house." I commented, tilting my head to take it all in.

"It used to be for mothers on campus," Syl explained. "But that was decades ago. You're not far off though. I think it's like six dorm rooms across both floors."

The *beep* of Syl's ID card snapped me out of my thoughts, and the door swung open. I felt like I was entering a new level of a video game signaling that I was about to dive into something new and unpredictable. At this point, I could hardly guess what Syl was leading me towards.

Inside, the air was thick and damp. Steam from the communal bathroom hung in the air, carrying the odd mix of coconut body wash and mildew. It wasn't pleasant, but it was like any other communal bathroom. Syl led the way up the stairs, knowing exactly where we were going and I didn't ask.

We reached a door. Syl didn't knock. She turned and smiled at me, wordlessly telling me to follow.

Inside, a girl sat at a desk, rolling a joint. Tattoos covered her arms, neck, even her feet. She looked rough— but in a way that said she didn't give a shit what you thought. Her sandy blonde hair was tied into a messy ponytail that suited her perfectly.

"Hey, Syl. Quarter, right?" she said flatly.

"Yeah," Syl replied, that mischievous grin on her face.

The girl's eyes moved to me, scanning me like I was

some unfamiliar object. I tried to hold her gaze, but my chest tightened, and I looked away.

"Who's this? A friend?"

"Yeah, she's cool. This is Edith."

Liz's expression didn't change as Syl leaned in and whispered something. She reached into a drawer and handed Syl a small jewelry bag filled with tiny slips of paper. The transaction happened so fast I almost missed it.

We left the room and stepped back into the cool air. I hadn't realized I was holding my breath until now.

Syl turned to me, her grin wide. "Care for a ride?"

"Where?"

"Nowhere in particular. You're with me—and you don't have a choice. Come on."

I jogged to catch up. That was always how it was with Syl—she moved at her own speed, and I had to keep pace. We reached a building that looked like a normal historic home. Syl pushed open the Dutch doors.

A student sat at a desk, eyes glued to her laptop.

"Can I help you?" she asked, not looking up.

"Two bikes, please."

She passed over a clipboard. Syl signed for us.

We dragged out two rusted bikes from a dorm storage closet through a basement kitchen. Syl insisted we start by coasting down the steep hill behind the underclassmen's dorms. The path was cracked from years of erosion, but that didn't stop her.

"Ready?" Syl called, already pushing off.

We sped downhill, wind tearing at our hair and drying out our mouths as we screamed. My handlebars shook beneath me, the wheels rattling, but I didn't care. We hit each bump with full laughter, coasting until we reached the bottom, skidding to a stop just shy of parked cars.

For a second, everything felt weightless. Like we were kids again—pedaling into summer, into nowhere.

Syl, as always, was the first to take off. I raced to keep up. We crossed a bridge, ducking under an old overpass, and coasted along a quiet greenway. The city faded into the background, hidden by trees with a few clinging leaves.

As we slowed down, I found myself lost in thought. It was almost too peaceful here for the heaviness I'd been feeling. The sunlight flickered through the branches, casting soft shadows on the fading grass.

I glanced at Syl, watching her ride beside me. So much had changed between us, yet riding together like this made me realize how much I clung to who we used to be. At twelve, neither of us had kissed anyone. Our desires back then were more straightforward—innocent. Everything felt complicated, and I craved things I couldn't have, unlike her, who seemed to get whatever she wanted.

Syl pulled off the path, leading us toward a quiet creek. We leaned our bikes against a tree and sat on the bank, cross-legged in the sand. She pulled out her rolling papers and began twisting a joint, her fingers working effortlessly. I couldn't stop watching them, mesmerized by how her hands moved.

"Bad luck, you know," I said as she pulled out a white lighter.

"Only if you believe it," she replied, exhaling smoke with a grin.

We passed it back and forth, letting the world fade. I

felt my muscles relax, tension melting for the first time in ages. With Syl, here, now—it was enough.

We stood. I put out the cherry in the sand and pocketed the filter. We looked into each other's red eyes, light with bliss. The landscape buzzed with color and energy. I felt alive.

A laugh bubbled out of me. Syl joined in. The moment wrapped us in freedom, in weightlessness, in light.

Dusting myself off, I called after her, "Where are we off to now?"

"Nowhere in particular," she said, pedaling faster, forcing me to keep up.

We zoomed along the road's walkway, the sharp breeze biting at my skin, when she suddenly veered off onto a practice soccer field and into a lightly wooded area. Signs of construction loomed ahead—orange cones and a giant sign that read *DANGER*, warning us to turn back. I didn't want to draw attention or risk getting in trouble, but curiosity pulled me forward. I kept trailing her, even though every instinct said this was a bad idea.

It always took effort for me to live in the moment like this. But Syl? She veered off paths without a second thought. She lived for whimsy, for chaos, while I could barely comprehend it.

Before long, we were beneath two tiers of highway. Overpasses loomed above, blocking out the sky. Syl slowed to a stop and dismounted. I followed, taking in the strange hush beneath the constant rumble of traffic.

"This where you take me to kill me?" I half-joked, though the air felt thick, unnatural.

Syl laughed, not even looking at me. "Oh, come on. Someone would find you eventually."

"True."

The sound of cars overhead vibrated the ground as she closed her eyes and tilted her face up toward the concrete. "I love it here when I need space. It's transcendent. Makes the real world feel both near and far, like I'm just this orb of energy soaking everything in."

"Smells funny, too," I muttered.

She whipped her head around, eyes flaring. "Laugh all you want, but some things exist beyond what we can see. We just don't *tap* into that part of our brains."

"Have you been drinking Hawaiian Lotus again?"

"So what if I have? You gonna judge me like you always do?"

She didn't let me answer. She pulled me into a quick embrace, a breathy chuckle escaping her. This was us— bickering, needling, challenging each other, never quite breaking the bond. It was what we did.

I loved her for it. And I hated it.

No matter how much I wanted her, she exhausted me with her intensity. Her mind was always somewhere bigger than here, reaching for the ineffable—and that scared me. I hugged her back, twisting a fistful of her shirt.

In that moment, I wondered if this would be our last trip together. I couldn't keep up with Sylvia Harrington anymore. No matter how much I loved her.

We broke apart. Syl smiled like nothing had shifted. I mirrored her, but something in me ached sharply. We could never hate each other—but we'd never be the same.

"Wanna go to the library?" she asked, suddenly

chipper. "They've got the comfiest chairs."

I nodded. The moment had already slipped away. We pedaled back toward campus. My chest leaden.

Returning the bikes was a pain in the ass. The hill up from the parking lot might as well have been Everest. By the time we locked them back in the closet, we were glistening with sweat and panting. I was relieved to find the library right next door.

Chapter Ten

We entered through the bottom floor, which housed a modest exhibit space—simple but charming displays of archival items and permanent collections. We climbed to the main floor.

Syl led me toward the computer lab. The ceilings startled me—they were massive compared to the cramped layout of the rest of campus. The building's unassuming exterior hadn't prepared me for the openness inside. Long windows flooded the space with too much light, even on an overcast day. The scent of stale books filled the air, mingling with the worn upholstery and wrinkled magazines.

"I need to finish a paper," Syl said, veering off. "Just footnotes and printing. Shouldn't take long—d'you mind?"

"Go ahead," I said, though she was already halfway gone.

I sat at the end of a long table, dust floating lazily in the air. I liked the stuffiness of old libraries—how they felt both vast and stifling, filled with knowledge and silence. It wasn't a *real* library unless the ventilation was terrible.

I pulled out my sketchbook and pen, working on the view outside the window. Scratchy hatch marks built up as I tried to capture the moment. I didn't know if Syl would take five minutes or twenty, so I let myself get lost in the motion of ink.

After a while, I glanced up. Syl wasn't writing. She was browsing online.

Typical slacker student. I wasn't judging before, but I am now.

With a sigh, I set my sketchbook aside and pulled out my journal. I needed to get something out:

It's our first full day together. Not exactly what I pictured. But a bike ride and getting high by the creek isn't the worst way to start. She'll never see me the way I see her, though...

I doodled in the margins, then tucked the journal away.

"I'm going to look around," I called to Syl, who was still absorbed in her phone.

"Wait—shit—hold on, I'll be done in—"

"It's alright," I cut in. "Take your time."

"You sure?"

"Yeah! I'll be back. Or you can find me in the stacks..."

Why did I say that?

"Edie..."

"Redact that. Okay. I'll be back now."

I turned away, eyes squeezed shut in embarrassment. I'd just made a love bid and got shut down with a single syllable. I started with the nonfiction section, but nothing caught my eye. Main floors never had anything good. All the carrels were occupied, every table full. Figures.

I found a separate stairwell and climbed to the fourth floor—home to the arts.

I'd never seen a collection like this. The culinary arts alone spanned multiple rows, sorted by country and subcategorized by method. Art history stretched endlessly—leather-bound classics on every master you could name and then some. A whole section was dedicated to Escher and Vivian Maier. My fingers brushed delicate bindings that felt ready to flake apart.

One book practically crumbled in my hands. The last stamp on the library card inside was from the 1970s. I flipped through, soaking in the smell of ink and time. When I snapped the book shut, a puff of dust enveloped me. I took a deep inhale.

If I die from toxic book dust, at least I'll die content.

Oddly, no one else was up here. The silence buzzed in my ears like noise-canceling headphones. Then again, why would artists be dedicated to the library when they should be working in the studio. Roaming the edge of the floor I found a carrel tucked into a mansard window. You could see the dust standstill in the air, it called to me. And when I peeked around, I found a book left open, not yet returned to its home on the shelf.

It had a solid coating of dust. Weird. Caked on to the point I couldn't make out the words on the page. I picked it up to blow the dust off and check the cover bound in cracked leather and there's no title on the cover or spine. No barcode. No catalogue number.

Flipping back to the page that it was opened to, the heading of a section reads, "Disciples Who Failed to Ascend."

What the fuck?

I flipped ahead—illustrations of women and girls, some fully detailed, others scratched out violently.

I dropped the book. It hit the floor with a sharp *thud*.

Syl's voice cut through the silence. "Find anything good?"

Heart pounding, I stuffed the book into my bag. As I did, she grabbed my wrist.

"What's that?"

"Nothing. I was just—putting away my sketchbook."

"Oh? Let me see!"

She let go, expectantly. I pulled out the sketchbook and zipped my bag nearly closed, flipping to the page I'd drawn earlier.

"Neat! Come on—I wanna show you something."

She grabbed my wrist again, pulling me toward the Art History section, deep into the dimming stacks. Letting go, she scanned the shelves.

"Ah! Here."

She pulled down a Hieronymus Bosch book and flipped straight to *The Garden of Earthly Delights*.

"I wasn't sure if he was still your favorite, but he's mine. Especially this piece."

Poser. "Yeah. Bosch is great," I said, feeling my shoulders tense.

She pointed out absurd little figures like we were playing *I Spy*, glossing over the symbolism, the deeper meanings. It felt hollow.

Before we left, I slid the library card out from the book's front cover. No one would miss it. I tucked it into my sketchbook—a keepsake for this moment.

Syl led us to the far end of the floor. We stood at a mansard window, overlooking the slope below. The campus dropped off like a cliff. The interstate from earlier was just a ribbon in the distance.

"The book selection sucks," Syl said, smiling. "But I love cramming here."

I looked at her, that ache rising again. "It's not bad."

She caught my gaze, her expression softening. "Remember our Reading Marathon weekends?"

"Yeah. I remember when you were Team Jacob in your *Twilight* phase."

"I miss those days. Just us. A book. No distractions. My best friend…"

"Don't get sentimental," I said, though it hurt to say it.

Syl shrugged, still looking at the view. "I want to take you to another library. You've seen most of campus already. This next one's better."

We stepped outside, breathing in the crisp air like it could clear the dust from our lungs. Instead of heading for the parking lot, Syl veered toward the Flats.

"Need to pop in. If you know what I mean."

"Not really."

She pulled out the tabs she'd bought from Liz.

"Now?"

"Don't be such a wimp. By the time you come down, it'll be midnight. You in or not?"

I hesitated. I needed something to dull the ache.

"I'm in."

Chapter Eleven

On second thought, there was no way I was doing this.

"Should we be doing this?" I asked.

"Why not?" Syl shot back without hesitation.

I paused. "Good point," I replied, stopping myself from becoming a total Debbie Downer.

"You've tripped before, right?" she asked, watching me fidget with the tab of acid between my fingers.

"Yeah, but—"

Syl rolled her eyes. "No buts. Don't be a prude. It's not as intense as they make it out to be. You can handle it. Now pop that shit and let's have a good time."

I hesitated, chewing on my lower lip. "What if I'm not alright?"

"Then make yourself alright, Aldridge."

I cringed. I'd never heard her use my last name like that—as a warning. She tried to soften her tone and added, "You'll be fine. Trust me. Take a second to collect yourself. But either way, we're going."

"I don't think I can handle being in public like this," I admitted, my voice shaky, a knot of anxiety already twisting in my chest. If this all goes wrong, if Mother finds out. No telling what she would do.

"Oh, no one cares. Don't act weird and you'll be fine. Plus, I've got a few more tabs, and we're not spending this break sober." She grinned, that maddeningly confident grin that always made me feel like nothing was impossible with her around.

"Yeah. Fuck it."

Fuck it... fuck it... FUCK IT!

I placed the tab on my tongue and closed my mouth like sealing a pact. The paper began to dissolve, bitter and faintly chemical, something foreign now inside me. I had to remind myself to breathe. Every exhale caught on the edge of panic.

Syl watched me like a proud mother hen. A proud hen who had just coaxed me into dropping acid.

I thought of the design on the tab—a potion bottle with swirling blue smoke, repeated Warhol-style. I imagined some wild-eyed madman with a Cheshire grin, dripping bright blue liquid into the vial, fully aware of its power and completely lost to the delusion.

"Alright," Syl chirped, yanking me from my spiral. "It'll take twenty minutes or so to kick in. It takes ten to get to the library."

She grabbed my arm, bouncing with excitement so infectious I almost forgot the dread clawing at my ribs.

Here we go.

I wondered if I'd regret this. As we got ready to leave, my mind ping-ponged between curiosity and worry. The tab was already dissolving.

Shit.

I was still coming down from the weed, and now I

had minutes—maybe seconds—before the trip took hold. That familiar tingling started in my gut, creeping up past my diaphragm, into my throat. I considered puking, but it was too late. The chemicals were in. No turning back.

I tried reframing it. Maybe it'd be fun. A story to tell later. I'd done shrooms, but acid? That was uncharted territory.

We lingered in the apartment longer than we probably should have. I could already feel it warming in my system. My skin buzzed, but the world hadn't shifted yet. Just nerves.

"Shouldn't we leave soon?" I asked, grasping for structure.

Syl waved me off. "Yeah, yeah. I was waiting on you. And before you bitch—I'm good to drive. Let's go."

Skeptical but compliant, I climbed into her silver Pontiac Vibe. It smelled like her—shampoo, perfume, a trace of weed. Like being wrapped in her essence. I fidgeted with the vents, my jacket, the seatbelt. Anything to ground myself.

She hit play on the stereo, and Mac Demarco's *Freaking Out the Neighborhood* filled the car. I let the music take over, sinking into the seat and focusing on the rhythm instead of my racing heart. As we drove, I stared at the rooftops and the sky, searching for the moment when the world would change.

We were nearly there and I was still waiting. We found a parking spot on campus. The lot was almost deserted. As I stepped out of the car, something shifted. The wind, the trees, the light... the world started to feel different. I looked up at the branches swaying above us, and the sky fractured into geometric patterns. Hexagons shimmered at the edge of my vision. Little flickers of energy bounced between everything. Trees and buildings weren't just still—they were *breathing.*

Syl caught me staring. "Kicking in?"

"I think so."

We kept walking. The air felt charged with possibility. Patterns wove themselves into every surface, every sound. Everything was so organized. Structured. Why had the world always *felt* chaotic when it clearly was not?

Everything fit. Perfectly. As if by design.

What did it mean that everything was exactly as it should be?

We walked into the library, hand in hand. The world swelled with energy, but Syl's presence kept me grounded. She led the way, ordering us coffee at Starbucks while I tried to blend in with the normalcy of it all.

She handed me gum.

"For your jaw. You're going to clench."

I nodded, trusting her. I would trust her always, even now, with this drug seeping into my brain and dissolving the edges of reality.

The high came quickly. It didn't feel like a door opening but like a shift in the entire structure of the room. The library wasn't just a building anymore—it was a portal.

I wasn't here to read. I was here to *unlock* something.

Letters floated off the pages in the periphery of my vision. They danced like stars, and I giggled. The shelves hummed, vibrating with hidden potential. I brushed my hand along the spines, and knowledge flooded me. I pulled back before it swallowed me whole.

"I could learn everything," I whispered.

Syl took my hand, pulling me deeper into the stacks.

We drifted through our own private dimension. Everything else fell away. People weren't people—just flickering orbs. Background noise.

Only Syl mattered. Her presence. Her touch. Her gravity.

Am I who I am because of me… or because of her?

She'd always known what to do. Had it all figured out. She could've done anything—*been* anything—and she would've done it perfectly. I was just… here. Hoping she'd keep pulling me forward.

We wandered until I collapsed into a chair. Patterns danced around me, everything shifting and glowing. I started sketching—chairs, shelves, light beams. Every line flowed with purpose.

"You're in your own world," Syl said, voice cutting through the current.

I looked up. She was clear. Real. The only real thing left.

"I checked the time," she whispered. "It's been hours."

"What?" I blinked. "It feels like… nothing."

"It's almost midnight. We have to go."

"No. I just started this." I gestured to my sketch. I wasn't ready to leave. I was *home* here—in the buzz of books, the hum of Syl's presence, the sense of rightness pulsing around me.

"We need a breather. Come on."

Reluctantly, I followed her, peeling myself away from the world I was building. We passed into another section of the library. Something shifted again. The windows overlooked the lawn—and the grass was rippling like water.

My stomach flipped.

Syl kept walking, but she was distant now, slipping away like a mirage. I couldn't reach her. I didn't know *where* she was.

The panic rushed in.

And just when it began to spiral—

She grabbed my wrist, tugging me forward through the exit.

"Don't leave me," I whispered.

She didn't hear me.

CHAPTER TWELVE

Before

I hoped Syl would come around sooner rather than later. There was no other path—I had to stay by her side, no matter what. We could rekindle the relationship, I know it. There's no future in my eyes where I don't see Syl there by my side. Doesn't she see us that way too? I couldn't even think about the answer and there was no way I would let our friendship fall off because her parents are ridiculous.

After a week or so, I was going insane. I had to get full context. One night of overthinking everything I trudged through boxes in the garage to find a pair of binoculars I forced my mother to buy at a yard sale years ago. Past me knew one day I would have to take matters into my own hands. There's no harm in just watching. It's not like I haven't been there before and don't know these people. Syl's family had a few acres and a patch of thick bamboo —great cover. It was so dense it felt like nighttime even during the day, if not for the swaying of the shallot leaves.

Once it got dark, the bamboo was too creepy, so I climbed one of the tall trees and stayed there for hours. Her parents came home in the early evening. Mrs. Harrington made dinner. They ate together *in silence. Later, they watched TV for two hours. Then, around nine, they all went their separate ways for the night.*

No answers tonight. I'd have to head back soon before my mom got worried. I figured I could reach my car and avoid the main roads—just cut through a stretch of woods for a couple of miles, make it home in time to eat whatever had been left in the microwave. It was already pitch-black and terrifying, but I had no choice. I'd parked off the shoulder, a white shirt hanging from the window as a marker. Next time I'd park down the neighboring driveway. The owner is a man in his eighties that never leaves; he shouldn't mind.

Yeah, I shouldn't miss anything. All her dad watches is Cops and expects them to watch it every night, enthralled by endless reruns. Even I would get roped in when we did hangout. Her father would always act like each traffic stop and runaway was a big case. It would surprise me every time when he would react by pounding the arm of the recliner. Her mother would go to fix him a second dinner to keep his mouth stuffed and give her a reprieve from watching the show. Syl would look out the living room window, unknowing that both of us were looking into each others eyes, bored out of our minds, wishing we were somewhere else.

Her dad had always been a dick. No surprise there. Sometimes, to avoid his drunken outbursts, they wouldn't even watch TV together. After a couple of warnings from the doctor, he got sober. But the fear of abandonment never left—just curdled into something sharper. His rage didn't stop; it crescendoed.

I often wondered what he was like when no one was watching. That's what fascinated me. Seeing the "unshakable" Mr. Harrington when he thought he was alone.

I panned my binoculars across the windows and found Sylvia's silhouette, thin and luminous in the lamplight of her room. I'd never done this before—spied like this. It was hard not to get too wrapped up in what everyone was doing. I didn't have a specific goal. I just wanted to understand what had become so private that I was suddenly no longer allowed to see her.

I told myself I'd only do it once. But that's how it always starts, right? I can't help it. It becomes compulsive. I have to be near my person or I'll disintegrate. The thought of their rejection would burn me alive. So I stay distant, but close. Safe—for both of us—until she's ready to accept me.

It's okay. I'm a patient person. I'm used to not getting my way.

Something in my bones thrummed, my intuition in full harmony. I know I'm manifesting what's meant to be. One day, she'll run to me. She'll say I was the one all along. We're in sync—on some cosmic wavelength no one else can access. We've found the doors into each other's psyche.

Over the course of two weeks, I learned her rituals. She'd take out her embroidery kit, thread a long needle, and poke her inner thigh. Then she'd smile, touch the skin around it carefully, never disturbing her "work." I counted—she did it daily. Always the same. Wait two minutes, swipe her middle finger through the wound to clean it, wipe it on her underwear. Then she'd touch herself. Gasp. Glance around.

I saw you, Syl.

She puts on a show for anyone willing to watch. It's not subtle. Her obsession with blood... maybe she doesn't see it as self-harm. Or maybe she doesn't care if someone assumes it is.

I imagined taking Syl on the kind of dates only I would know to take her on—candlelight dinner in an empty field. Somewhere open, I want Nox to be a witness to the body of a goddess that she could never hold a candle to. The flicker of fire between us will ignite her senses.

She'll compare me to Klimt's Danae. You won't have to hide

anymore, Sylvia. We will be able to join in a new way no one else has heard of, no walls between us. She must know I would do anything for her; we are meant to be together.

When the world around me turns into woods, and I realize that I'm not inside Sylvia's bedroom, the sting of reality bites. The cool night made everything even more uncomfortable. What are you doing to me, Syl?

Shifting my binoculars to the lower floor, I see her parents in the living room. It looks like they're about to go to bed. I don't understand why they have so many blankets for three people. They folded them, placed them in a neat pile on a chair. When Mrs. Harrington stood, she dropped her top in front of her husband. Her breasts were bare, unmarked by tan lines—probably from the tanning booth in their basement.

Yeah. I wasn't sticking around to watch old people fuck.

When I got home, I felt... conflicted. Disgust and euphoria, tangled together. This wasn't an either/ or situation. Honestly, it was more thrilling than actually being at a sleepover. But I only step into the darkness to see what needs to be seen—and then I get the fuck out.

I know there are consequences. I'm not an idiot. I can't make this a habit. They only need to catch me once, and I'm finished. I set out to watch Syl because I care about her. I'm not letting her disappear just because her dad chased me off the porch a few times.

That night, I couldn't sleep. Guilt coiled in my chest. I picked up one of my "soft" books—low angst, high romance—to try and reset. I imagined Syl and me together, trying to scrub the image of her parents from my mind.

It didn't work. I tried another book.

Throughout the year, I keep my reading balanced: some Homer, a little Kafka, maybe a dark romance here and there depending on my mood. I grabbed the Kierkegaard, mostly because I knew I wouldn't get past the first chapter.

Still couldn't sleep.

After an hour, I gave up. I did a few stretches, climbed out the second-story window, and shimmied down the trellis.

And I went back.

The adrenaline of returning to the Harrington house was intoxicating. My blood pulsed in my ears, louder than the car engine. I wasn't at the Harringtons, but I was there. Nothing had changed. Twilight had done nothing good for me.

There was a rhythm now. A groove. Just me, in a tree, with my binoculars. Yeah, it's very peeping-Tom of me—I know. But this is a rural mountain town, not suburbia. Even with their porch lights, they'd never see me.

One night, Mr. Harrington went off the rails. I saw him get up from the recliner and start moving frantically, yelling at his wife and daughter. It's pathetic for a man to treat his spouse like a slave. The nerve it takes to yell at others over every small problem. I think the most I've gotten out of the weeks of watching is that Mr. Harrington is a pathetic little man who will never understand what it means to please a woman. That's why Mrs. Harrington fucks the pool boy every chance she can. A girl has to live, I guess. If I were her, I would have snapped by now and poisoned him slowly over time. I would imagine the moments following him striking you, and thought about how it would be an obvious self-defense and easy out. Another thing I've learned is why your spouse is statistically the most likely to kill you. It's deeper than 'Sorry, I'm too much of a coward to get a divorce. I have to kill you.' 'It's not my fault you cheated. You must die.'

If only humans were that simple. I wish there was something more to watch than Mr. Harrington be the classic horrible authoritative alcoholic father. Like clockwork, I'll see Sylvia run upstairs. Shut her door turning the knob to prevent any sound, even though I know she wants to slam it to expel the rage. I used to envy her life, but over time I've come to have sympathy for her. Even more when I noticed her get into bed for the night, and I don't know why but I stayed. I kept watching for hours and it paid off. Because I soon saw none other than Mr. Harrington go inside of her bedroom, watching her sleep, and eventually some unspeakable things I wouldn't wish onto anyone. More than once.

Without her fucking knowledge.

A few nights later, Syl waited for hours before sneaking out. She climbed from her window, scaled the porch posts, and dropped down silently. We used to sneak out together—she knew how to do it. The trick was to push the car in neutral to the end of the driveway. This time, she had to do it alone. It took her twenty minutes, dragging the car backwards foot by foot, sweat glistening in the porch light. She didn't know I was watching.

But I was.

Where are you going, Sylvia?

Chapter Thirteen

I zoned out for most of the ride back to the Flats. My mind felt eerily serene, like my thoughts had unspooled and were drifting on a breeze. I leaned my head against the cool glass of the backseat window, but my brain was elsewhere—detached, but not quite free.

"I read this book once about a guy who was a brain surgeon," I said, unsure if I was talking to anyone in particular. "He said the brain actually feels like toothpaste."

Silence stretched in the car, thick and heavy. No one responded. I didn't mind. I wasn't even sure I was looking for an answer.

Emberly drove without speaking, but her eyes darted toward Sylvia. I couldn't tell if it was pity, concern, or anger. Maybe all three. Her aura prickled the skin on my arms.

We pulled into the small parking lot behind the Flats, the car settling into stillness. Finally, Emberly spoke—her voice sharp enough to slice through the quiet.

"Syl, why would you do this while your friend's visiting? Seriously? What the fuck."

Sylvia curled up tighter against the window, arms wrapped around herself. "More like an acquaintance," she muttered, her voice distant. "Come on, you know we hardly know each other anymore…"

Emberly shot me a look—half pity, half triumph—before twisting it into a smile. "Right. But if she acts a fool, it's you who takes the fall. I don't care what she does. It's you I care about."

I went speechless. Her words landed like a punch to the chest. My mind froze, teetering on the edge of too many emotions. I didn't move. I waited for them to open their doors, half-expecting Emberly to confess her love to Sylvia while she was at it. I lagged behind, needing a second to gather myself unnoticed.

Inside the kitchen, the soft yellow stove light wrapped the room in a warm glow. My eyes wandered up to the wooden beams overhead, tracing the knots and swirls in the grain. There was something soothing about it—but also nauseating. Like the world was trying to offer comfort only to spin me in the opposite direction the moment I looked too closely.

Emberly stood from rummaging in the fridge, face tight, the bridge of her nose wrinkled.

"Y'all up for getting some pizza?" she asked. "You need food in your system. Trust me."

"We're fine," Sylvia and I answered in unison.

Emberly raised a brow and pointed at both of us. "No, you're not. You haven't eaten, and if you don't, you'll regret it. Let's go."

I blinked, trying to readjust to reality. "Didn't we just get back?"

"Yep," Sylvia replied, already walking to the door.

"If you need to use the bathroom, go ahead. We'll wait," Emberly said, her voice softening as she turned toward me.

"Right. I'll be quick," I muttered, disappearing down the narrow hallway into the half-bath. The mirror stared back, warped in the yellow hue of the dying lightbulb. I splashed cold water on my face to ground myself. My reflection shifted—freckles forming patterns, eyes swirling like a lava lamp. My body didn't feel real.

Who are you? The thought slipped through my mind like smoke.

"EDIE! YOU COMING?" Sylvia's voice shattered the spell.

I took a breath, adjusted my clothes, and reentered the kitchen, avoiding eye contact as I joined them.

"You good? That took forever," Emberly teased as we stepped outside.

"Got lost in my own eyes," I said flatly.

Sylvia snorted. "Modest as always."

We piled back into the car, the city's glow wrapping around us like a blanket. I leaned back, watching rooftops glide past under the soft wash of streetlights. My mind stayed quiet, a strange calm blooming in my chest. For the first time in a while, I felt… free. Maybe Sylvia was out of my hands. Maybe it was time to stop trying so hard to be liked.

We reached the pizza place quickly. Its red neon sign bathed the sidewalk in light, the scent of cheese and fresh dough spilling into the air.

Emberly glanced at us, assessing whether we could

hold it together.

Inside, the shop was a comforting blend of tacky and nostalgic. Neon lights flickered overhead, casting shadows over framed photos of Little League teams. I rubbed my temples and tried to adjust. This place and the diner back home could've been twins—unpretentious, familiar. No judgment. That was rare.

Emberly took charge and ordered a cheese pizza and a bacon-and-pineapple one. I leaned against the counter, watching the chef toss dough in smooth, practiced arcs. His movements had rhythm, almost like a performance, but I was too tired to lose myself in it.

I didn't realize I was hungry until the smell hit. My stomach growled. Emberly handed me a Diet Coke, which I drank too fast. The cold fizz numbed my throat, but I kept drinking, craving something solid—something real.

When the pizzas were ready, we took them back to the car. As we pulled away from the city center, Emberly spoke up.

"You good, Ed?"

I blinked. "Ed?"

"Yeah. Short, sweet, simple. Just like you," she smirked.

I wasn't sure if it was an insult or a compliment. I let it go. Emberly had been decent all night. Maybe I didn't need to dissect everything.

As we pulled into the dorm lot, Emberly's expression shifted like she'd just had an idea. She grabbed the pizzas and motioned for us to follow. We climbed up to the roof, sitting on the flat surface with the whole city stretched out before us. My heart thudded—was this safe right now? I pushed the thought down.

The pizza anchored me. I bit into a slice, warm cheese stretching and melting across my tongue. The simple act of eating brought me back to earth. I exhaled slowly, letting the peace settle.

"This doesn't look like regular pizza," I said between bites.

We laughed—really laughed. Our voices floated into the night air, echoing off rooftops. For the first time in forever, I let myself ease into the moment. I still had a thousand questions—but for now, they could wait.

CHAPTER FOURTEEN

Before

I had been watching her family for a few months now, and I was starting to lose hope. The pangs in my chest grew sharper every time I imagined Syl finding out what I'd been up to—knowing I had seen things she believed were private, watching her when she thought she was alone. It felt like cheating, but my need to win her over always outweighed logic and reason. I didn't realize it then, but it was the calm before the storm. Autumn of our senior year was the most relaxing part of high school since we reunited. Football games, late nights at arcades, cruising through town with poorly wrapped joints like no time had passed. We got over the hurdle of not staying the night, more like I did, but managed to spend all hours of the evening together. I respected her wishes and thought it would help me repress my feelings anyways.

Sylvia and I were more stressed and pulling our hair out over college applications anyways. Bigger fish to fry. Most nights when we could barely read the words on our screens, we threw on slippers and dragged ourselves to the local gas station. I'd kick my feet up on the dash, tearing into mozzarella sticks, stretching the cheese as high as

I could like it was some kind of test—and every time, Sylvia's eyes were elsewhere. Scanning the lot for druggies or watching couples make out in their trucks.

Whenever we spotted a guy pawing at his girlfriend like he was trying to peel her open, we'd burst into laughter.

"He's gonna rip her tit off before their first date's even over," I'd say, and Sylvia would giggle, shaking her head.

We'd place bets on whether he even bought her a drink. We laughed at how fast those romances would burn out.

Just us. A gas station parking lot. Suspended in time.

For once, I wasn't thinking about what came next.

Until Sylvia finished her food and said, "I better get home. My mom and dad are probably waiting."

Her mom didn't care. I knew that. It was her dad. Always her dad. Sinking his claws in deeper, dragging her further from me. Tonight I'd had enough. Graduation was looming. My time was running out.

"Syl... do you think we'll still be friends after all this?"

She didn't look at me. Her gaze stayed on the teenagers loitering in the lot, like she could see everyone's future but her own.

"I don't know. Maybe. But that's not how life works," she said. "People have expectations. And I'm not sure I'll live up to any of them. Why worry about it when we can just live for right now?"

"And right now?" I asked.

She licked her ice cream cone slowly, absentmindedly. "Right now... I wonder if you'd kiss a girl for a thousand dollars."

I frowned. "Yeah. I mean, it's just a kiss. Wouldn't you?"

Sylvia wrinkled her nose. "No. Gross."

The word hit like a slap. Whether she knew or not—maybe she did—it didn't matter.

"How is that gross?"

"I don't have anything against being gay," she said, finishing her cone. "It's just not for me. I can't even imagine kissing a girl without cringing."

"I see," I said, swallowing the sting. My throat tightened.

She leaned back in her seat, casting me a sideways glance with a crooked smirk. "Maybe I'd kiss you... if I were drunk enough."

"Real nice," I muttered. "You already sound drunk—and you're supposedly straight."

Sylvia turned, her eyes sharp. "Excuse me?"

"You heard me," I said, though I immediately shrank into the seat, regretting every word. I didn't know what I'd just opened.

The silence that followed was taut and electric. Finally, she let out a breath and turned back to the parking lot. Her expression inscrutable.

I stared out the window, my chest aching. I couldn't shake the rejection. The sharp, familiar pain of watching Sylvia look at everyone but me. The late-night talks, the shared laughter, the subtle touches—they weren't what I needed them to be. I longed for her in a way she wouldn't—or couldn't—see.

It was always the same cycle. I let myself get swept up in the moment. A glance. A smile. A shared laugh. And then she'd say something that shattered the illusion. Reality would crash back in.

She always reminded me, one way or another, that nothing would ever happen between us.

And yet—I always came back. No matter how much it hurt, I couldn't let her go.

We sat in silence, eating what was left of our snacks. When I glanced over, Sylvia was watching a group of rednecks. The kind she always noticed. A sharp, white-hot wave of jealousy pulsed through me. It wasn't just that she looked at them. It was that she never looked at me.

"*Where are we going?*" *I asked, startled by the car engine roaring to life.*

"*You'll see,*" *she said, smirking again.*

She drove us behind the local library. The lot was dark and empty. My breath hitched. My cheeks flushed. The air was heavy, charged with something unspoken.

She turned off the engine but kept her hands on the steering wheel, like she needed something to hold onto. Then she slowly turned to face me. Her breathing was shallow. The silence between us swelled, thick with tension.

I cleared my throat. "Are you okay?"

She swallowed hard. "I just wanted to... not tell you, but…"

I reached out, resting my hand on her arm. She was trembling.

"*Syl, whatever it is—*"

"*I'm pregnant.*"

My stomach dropped. "What?"

She burst out laughing, shaking her head. "No. I'm not. But you should've seen your face."

Before I could react, Sylvia leaned in and kissed me. It was quick—almost too fast to register—but the feel of her lips stayed with me, imprinted.

"*What the—*" *I started, but she cut me off.*

"*Don't tell anyone. Or I'll tell everyone you're gay for me.*"

I stared at her, heart hammering. For a second, the whole world tipped sideways. Then, without thinking, I reached for her, pulling her close and kissing her back with everything I'd been holding in for years. I poured it all into that kiss—the longing, the obsession, the hope. I wanted to brand her with it, make it unforgettable. Make her remember me.

When I finally pulled away, Sylvia looked dazed. Her cheeks were flushed, her lips swollen. She reached beneath her seat and pulled out a bottle of whiskey, taking a long swig.

The moment was already slipping through my fingers.

I watched her drink as the heat in my body began to fade.

"That was nice," I said, trying to steady my voice. "You're a good kisser."

Sylvia laughed too loudly. "Nice? Please. I've had plenty of practice."

Her words stung, but I swallowed it. Played it cool.

"Yeah. I guess you have."

She handed me the bottle, and I took a long drink, feeling the alcohol burn its way down, taking the edge off the confusion and anger swirling inside me. I looked out the window, biting back the darker thoughts creeping in—thoughts of other people who had touched her, kissed her, tasted her.

"Come here," she said suddenly, her voice softer, edged with something I couldn't name.

I folded my arms, forcing a smirk. "Need more practice?"

She smiled with those puppy-dog eyes—the ones that always made me cave.

"Yeah. It's my first time kissing a girl."

Hearing that out loud hit me like a drug. Her first time.

I couldn't stop myself.

I lunged at her again, this time kissing her harder. Pouring years of silence and aching into the space between us. Her body softened beneath mine, responding with hesitant, hungry heat. For a moment, it felt like I was exactly where I was supposed to be.

But it wasn't real. It never was.

When I bit her lip too hard and tasted blood, she shoved me off with a gasp.

"Edith! What the hell?"

I blinked, stunned. "Sorry... I didn't mean—"

"Yes, you did!" she snapped. Her voice sharp, her eyes glassy with hurt and fury. The sting in her expression hit me harder than her push.

I could still taste her—salt and copper. And for a second, something twisted in my chest. A dark satisfaction. She had been mine. If only for a second.

But it passed. Quickly. Shame bloomed in its place.

I reached for her, instinctively, desperate to fix it—but she recoiled, hand pressed to her mouth.

"Don't touch me," she said, voice cracked, hitting me harder than her shove ever could.

I sat there, staring at her, my body still humming from the kiss, my fingers tingling with the need to touch her again. But my mind was a mess of regret and something darker, something that still wanted more. I could feel the heat in my body cooling, but the need lingered, crawling under my skin.

Sylvia turned away, hands shaking as she fumbled for the whiskey bottle. She took another swig, her lips pressed so hard to the glass I thought it might break. A small part of me wanted to taste it again.

She wiped her mouth and glared at me.

"You're psycho."

I opened my mouth to apologize, but nothing came. Just silence. Thick and bitter.

She started the car and drove me home.

Neither of us spoke. We returned to the same silence we always did. The kind that never really left, no matter what we said or did.

Chapter Fifteen

With a start, I sat up in bed, skin prickling with that unmistakable feeling of being watched. My head throbbed, too big for my skull, and my stomach twisted with that familiar churn of unease. I blinked several times, clearing my vision—there was a figure standing in the doorway. I could've sworn I locked the door before bed. Maybe I hadn't.

I rubbed my eyes and squinted. "Harriet? You okay?"

Her eyes—dark, bottomless—were focused on something beyond me, unblinking.

"I'm fine."

"Need something?"

"Everyone else declined brunch at the Rat. Want to join me?"

Her voice was calm, but her posture—rigid, expectant—betrayed something else. Like she was holding her breath, waiting for an answer that mattered more than it should.

"Sure. Let me get ready real quick."

She gave a stiff nod and vanished down the hall without another word, leaving behind a silence so thick it felt like it had weight.

I changed in a daze, swapping pajama shorts for jeans, slipping into my white Adidas. But when I glanced in the mirror, something about my reflection looked... wrong. Slightly off. My body felt unfamiliar too, like I was wearing someone else's skin.

I shut the door, needing a moment alone. I rummaged through my pack until I found the book. I flipped through it desperately, seeking anything that could explain what the hell was happening. The pages were mostly diagrams—rituals, maybe—written like an instruction manual. One was circled in pencil: *Day Invited.* Beneath it, in faded ink, it read:

"To offer what cannot belong is to restore balance. Order through blood. Discord through invitation."

I kept flipping. The writing on most pages was ancient, barely legible. Then a slip of paper fluttered out and landed in my lap—new, bright white, with one word written in sharp blue ink:

Garrett.

My stomach dropped. Garrett—the missing day student. Was this a template? Were they still doing this? Why would an all-girls school have anything to do with him? The handwriting was definitely feminine. I had to find out what happened.

When I stepped out, Harriet was waiting in the living room, absorbed in her book. She looked serene, like the embodiment of a quiet fall morning, her honey-colored turtleneck matching the golden sunlight streaming through the windows. She reminded me of the trees I'd seen on the way here, bright and warm in a way that felt foreign to me.

I glanced at the cover of her book. "*White Nights*... any good?"

She closed the book, marking her spot with a careful thumb. "I can't put it down."

I nodded, suddenly unsure what to say. "I'm ready. You good?"

Outside, the morning was still half-asleep. Fog hovered low to the ground, and the sun cut through it with blinding sharpness. Harriet moved like she wasn't walking but gliding—hands clasped behind her back, eyes unfocused.

We passed the cemetery. The headstones stood like silent witnesses. Harriet looked at them but said nothing.

She insisted on using a meal voucher at the dining hall for me.

"You don't have to," I said quickly. "I can pay."

"Allow me." Her smile was soft, but something unreadable flickered behind her eyes as she handed the voucher to the cashier—her gaze never leaving mine.

The food was standard—bagels, waffles, sausage, pizza. My stomach ached, though I couldn't tell if it was from hunger or dread. I piled a bit of everything onto my plate. We sat at one of those oversized round tables meant for groups. The setup felt strange.

"Bit odd not to have smaller tables, don't you think?"

"Not really," Harriet replied, spooning yogurt into her mouth. "Women group together when men aren't around. By midday, this room will be full."

I glanced around, suddenly more aware of the space. The high ceilings, the chandeliers. The green walls and patterned carpet made it feel like a parlor from another era. Stained glass at the top of the arches painted the table in gentle reds and golds.

"Do you read much, Edith?" Harriet asked, her voice pulling me back.

"Not as much as you, clearly," I said, picking at my food. "You seem brilliant."

She smiled faintly. "You think so?"

"Definitely."

She looked at me for a long moment before speaking again. "You're quite smart, Edith."

I blinked, taken aback by the compliment. "How do you figure that?"

She shrugged, her eyes distant. "I can feel it."

I wasn't sure what to make of that, but I accepted the compliment and continued eating silently. We finished up, grabbed coffee, and headed back outside. The fog had lifted, but the air still felt thick with something unspoken.

"Mind if we stop by the bakery?" Harriet asked.

"Sure," I said. "As long as it's not the roof of a building, I'm good."

We wandered toward the square, and my eyes drifted to the library and back to Harriet, "Hey, how late is the library open here?"

"It's twenty-four seven." She offered as she disappeared into the bakery, leaving me outside to breathe in the scent of fresh bread. When she returned, she held a loaf of rosemary garlic bread and a tube of cookies. She popped the lid and offered one.

Her eyes gleamed with something I couldn't name.

I bit into the cookie—and moaned without meaning

to. It was absurdly good. Crisp, lemony, buttery. The kind of thing that made you question every dessert you'd ever called "great."

"Damn. That's good."

Harriet's smile deepened, but she said nothing. We walked in silence, our footsteps soft against the stone path.

As we passed the cemetery again, I spoke.

"They sort the graves. By gender, time of death— even marriage. And yet they're all flat stones, like it's supposed to be egalitarian. It feels... contradictory."

Harriet tilted her head, eyes scanning the graves.

"Maybe. Or maybe it's meant to say that in the end, we're all the same. Despite our differences, we return to the same place."

Her tone unsettled me. "Do you really believe that?"

Her smile wavered. "In the end, we're all just echoes. Some are louder than others. But even the loudest fade."

A chill ran through me, though I tried to brush it off. Harriet had a way of making even the most benign thoughts sound ominous.

Back at the Flats, the house was quiet. Harriet said no one would be up until two. I found *The Secret History* in a pile near the fireplace and curled up in the window seat. The light filtering through the leaves cast soft, dappled shadows across the room. For once, I felt still.

A few minutes later, Harriet brought tea. The scent of black tea and cardamom filled the room. She handed me a mug.

"Thank you," I said, taking a sip. "This is amazing."

She smiled, curling into her chair with her own book. The soft sound of violin played in the background. The quiet surrounded me like a cocoon. I sank into the cushions, lulled by the warmth.

I fell asleep.

When I woke, panic gripped me instantly. The room had shifted. The light outside the window was gone, replaced by a strange, cloying twilight that shimmered in hues no real sky would ever wear.

How long had I been asleep?

My heart raced as I got up, but the room felt wrong, stretched out in strange angles. The ticking clock in the foyer echoed loudly, slow and deliberate, each tick like a heavy thud in my chest.

Tick... tock...

The whispers started then, faint at first, like distant murmurs I couldn't make out. They weren't coming from the clock—they were upstairs. My feet moved independently, pulling me toward the sound, each step heavier than the last.

The stairs creaked under my weight, the wood groaning like it was alive. My breath hitched as I reached the top. I couldn't shake the feeling that something was horribly wrong.

The whispers grew louder. I couldn't make out the words, but they were close.

The door to Sylvia's room was slightly ajar.

Inside, I saw them—Emberly and Sylvia—tangled together. Moving in sync. Moaning.

I backed away, bile rising in my throat. I barely made it to the bathroom before I dry-heaved into the sink. Gripping the edge of the counter, I looked up—and froze.

My reflection was grinning.

But I wasn't smiling.

***

I shot upright on the couch, heart racing. The light outside the window had barely shifted. It was still midday.

The smell of burnt paper assaulted my senses while the bell chimed the hour in the distance, but the mantel clock read seven minutes after one. Wrong. Again. I'm definitely awake now.

Harriet still sat in her chair, entirely unfazed.

"You were dreaming a lot," she said, not looking up.

"How long was I out?"

"Maybe an hour and a half," she said. "One full REM cycle, I'd say."

I rubbed my eyes. "Did you do something to my tea?"

She smiled faintly. "I don't know what you mean."

I didn't press. I got up and slipped into the bathroom under the stairs. I splashed cold water on my face, but my reflection still didn't feel like mine.

When I returned to the kitchen, the smell hit me first—something savory in a slow cooker. Steam curled from the lid. My stomach growled despite the nausea lingering in my chest.

I reached for the lid—and felt a jab in my side.

I yelped, turning just as Emberly smirked at me, wielding meat claws.

"What the fuck, Emberly?"

She leaned against the counter. "Serves you right for snooping."

My face flushed. My heart raced, unsure if from fear, shame, or something else.

"Chill out, Ed," she teased, but there was something in her voice—low and sharp—that made my skin crawl.

"I wasn't snooping."

She laughed, turning back to the stove like it was nothing. "Sure you weren't."

I stood there, my heart racing, trying to piece together my thoughts. The touch had been light, but it had sent me a spasm of something electric. It didn't feel like a joke—but I had to give benefit of the doubt.

I could feel the weight of her eyes on me even as I left the room. I could hear the squelching of her pulling the meat apart as I walked away. My head was buzzing, thoughts crescendoing out of control.

The knot in my chest tightened, and my vision became blurry. I clenched my fists, trying to slow my breathing.

After a few moments, I stood by the window, staring out at the sun setting behind the trees. The horizon's purples and oranges faded into the night's deep blue, and everything outside felt... unreal. Like it was happening to someone else.

I took a swig from the wine Emberly had handed me earlier. It was sharper than expected—dry and bitter—but I kept drinking, hoping it would numb whatever was clawing at the edge of my thoughts.

Sylvia. Emberly. Harriet. Penelope.

They swirled around me, a constellation of things I couldn't decipher.

And I was unraveling, piece by piece.

And I didn't know how to stop.

Chapter Sixteen

Despite Penelope's encouragement, I slumped on the couch, drowning myself in wine. I could feel warmth blooming inside me—the version of myself that others seemed to like, coaxed out by the alcohol. But I pushed it down again when the church bell gave its ritualistic chime. Ten 'til.

I squinted at the wall clock, then up at the popcorn ceiling, tracing abstract shapes in the textured plaster. Time slipped away—an hour vanished before I realized it.

There was a man in the ceiling. Odd-looking. Handlebar mustache. His face came together in the dots and bumps above me, though I knew I could never draw it if handed a pen. I blinked, and Harriet's soft voice pulled me from the haze.

"Dinner's ready."

I sat up too fast. The room tilted, the edges of my vision wobbling like I was walking sideways. My stomach lurched—another reminder of how much I'd had to drink. I gripped the wineglass tighter and steadied myself before standing.

Not wanting to stumble in drunk, I ducked through

the hallway, topped off my glass with more wine. Just a little more. I took a breath and stepped into the dining room—only to see something I wish I hadn't.

Emberly kissed her. On the lips.

Just a soft, casual thing—like they did it all the time.

No one batted an eye. But my stomach twisted, sharp and cold, like dry ice searing through my chest. I tried to swallow it down, but my throat kept closing. I took a gulp of wine, trying to dissolve the lump. Instead, I choked—wine hitting the wrong pipe. I coughed so hard it set my nerves on fire. All eyes turned to me. Watching. Silent. Like I was something under glass.

"Wrong pipe," I muttered, laughing weakly, forcing a smile as I waved them off and slipped toward the hallway bathroom. Sylvia was on my heels, catching my elbow and turning me toward her.

"Can we talk?" she mumbled, glancing back at Emberly still bustling in the kitchen.

"What do you want?" I asked, brittle.

"I want to know what's wrong."

"It's her, isn't it? Why you're so distant. I guess I don't know you anymore," I said, swiping at the tear that escaped before I could stop it.

Syl rolled her eyes and sighed. "Just stop. You're being so possessive. Have you not changed at all since high school? Get over it. We haven't even spoken in years."

I said nothing, blinking hard, reaching for the doorknob, desperate to escape.

But she twisted me back around. "Look, I'm sorry. I just... I still have resentment. I need to let it go."

She stepped closer and whispered, "No one can

replace you, Edie. You have my heart, okay?"

Before I could respond, she looked both ways, then cupped my face gently in both hands and kissed me. Soft. Intentional.

She kissed *me*.

I didn't even open my eyes. I wanted more. Needed more.

Her hands flattened on my chest—stopping me, hard.

"We can't go further than that," she said softly.

"Syl, can I ask you one thing?"

"Yeah?"

"Are you single? Or not?" I wanted to confess to her, right now. I think it's the time, just rip it off like a bandaid. If she was willing to kiss me that has to count for something right?

"Depends." She alludes and turns to leave before I can react.

When I could finally enter the restroom I kept repeating to myself that I don't care, but I fucking do. My brain couldn't stop rambling a bunch of questions I would have asked to her vague response.

Depends? On what? The anxiety crescendoed , drowning out everything else. I tried to ground myself—focus on what I could control. I relieved myself, washed my hands, and stared into the mirror like it could give me an answer. I knew what I had to do. I had to tell her how I felt before I left.

When I stepped out from beneath the stairs, the dining room was fully transformed. It looked like something out of a period film—perfectly arranged, too flawless to be real. A moss-green runner stretched across the mahogany table. Silver gleamed in the candlelight. It didn't feel real. It didn't feel like it was meant for me.

In the center was a pot roast, crowned with a golden apple carved into a flower. The fat glistened, pooling around potatoes and carrots arranged with care. The scent enveloped me—rich, warm, homey.

But what caught my eye were the oranges. Scattered around the roast, bright and acidic. A strange detail—but somehow perfect. They'd cut the richness, balance everything out.

My stomach growled.

The women moved easily around the table, drifting through one another's space like they'd done it a thousand times. They grazed on pomegranate seeds and sliced apples, brushing fingertips as if it were second nature. There were no boundaries between them. The warmth was tangible.

I couldn't stop watching Sylvia—the way she moved, the way she lit up a room. Not just mine, but everyone's. That glow was never just for me.

They returned to their food, but my heart kept hammering in my chest. I glanced at Sylvia. She didn't notice. She never noticed. Emberly didn't either. They had already moved on, laughing at something Penelope said while I sat there attempting to school my features.

I felt Harriet's hand on my elbow. I cringed, her touch startling me more than I'd like to admit. Her grip was light, but something about it made me uneasy. I turned to look at her, forcing my breath to steady.

"Do you like it?" she asked, her eyes like toffee,

almost too inviting.

I blinked, trying to shake off the dizziness that lingered. "Are you serious?"

Harriet smiled, tilting her head just so, "Most of the time."

I let out a small, breathless laugh. "It's everything."

Harriet's smile widened, her eyes twinkling like I'd said exactly what she wanted to hear. For a moment, I felt like I belonged—like I *wanted* to belong. But something about it still felt... off.

We sat. The appetizers dwindled. Conversation flowed like a river I couldn't step into. I watched them: Penelope cackling, Harriet's knowing glances, Emberly and Sylvia caught in their own orbit. Everything that had happened kept spinning in my head. Harriet's strange intensity. Emberly's bite. Sylvia's hot-and-cold shuffle. I couldn't untangle it. I felt sick trying.

As one, they lifted their glasses. I followed.

Together, they spoke:

"To the Goddess who sees all and holds the balance. We eat in your name, in your favor, in your shadow. Let our voices rise, let our bonds strengthen. And let those unworthy be cast aside. To Discordia."

They drank. Then stared at me.

I raised my glass.

"To Discordia," I echoed.

And drank.

My mind went blank. What the hell was I doing?

I couldn't tell if it was chronic loneliness or the Sylvia of it all that made me crave their approval. Maybe both. You hear about these things. But when it's happening to *you*—it's harder to call it what it is.

I just didn't want to be sent home. Not yet.

At least they looked pleased.

Penelope broke into laughter. "Damn, Em! This could pass for a still life! Should we grab easels instead of plates?"

I smiled, even as the knot in my chest pulled tighter.

"I'm dead," Penelope wheezed, wiping her eyes.

Emberly leaned back, smirking. "That would be fun, don't you think, Syl? Harriet, you could take a break from your Petri dishes and channel your inner Renaissance woman."

"I do partake in embroidery on occasion," Harriet said calmly, a glint in her eye.

Penelope snorted. "Someone get this bitch a pillow to stitch, I need this moment immortalized!"

I kept watching Sylvia. She was eyeing the end piece of the roast—the one with the blackened edge and crisp vegetables. Of course she wanted it.

Penelope noticed too. "Look at Syl, already planning her attack."

Sylvia's eyes flicked to mine for a second. She said nothing, but I could feel the quiet challenge there. Her eyes returned to the roast, but the moment stretched longer than needed.

Harriet's tender voice sliced through the moment, "Why don't we let Edith go first? She's the guest of honor."

I stood slowly, the knife cold and heavy in my hand. Sylvia's eyes were on me, following every move I made. My heart pounded in my chest, my pulse quickening as I went to the roast. I didn't need to look at the meat to know which piece Sylvia wanted. The same one I'd noticed.

I hesitated for a second, my fingers tightening around the knife. Then I shoved it into the end piece, lifting it carefully onto my plate. Her face was forward, but her eyes were looking into me. And that fucking smirk, I didn't know what it meant, but it sent a chill down my spine nonetheless. What has this school done to her? The Syl I knew of didn't care for games, but I seemed to play into all of her schemes. Harriet and Penelope seemed to enjoy the silent standoff. As I finished serving myself Emberly stood, taking my plate as I was about to fork my first bite and threw it against the wall.

Penelope's snorted laugh broke the silence, but it barely registered.

Emberly's voice cracked like a whip:

"When we said you should go first, we didn't mean indulge. We meant you fucking serve us."

Sylvia chimed in, cool as ice. "You shouldn't have done that if you wanted to be one of us. You *do*, don't you?"

"Yes," I whispered. It sounded like begging.

"Then you should've known—being the guest of honor means you serve *us*. You get the apple. And we'll call it even."

I couldn't look her in the eye as I reached for the apple in the center.

"Gluttonous pig," she added. "Let's just hope you don't fall from grace again."

I took a bite.

It was good. But it wasn't pot roast and endless

perfect sides. Even with my plate shattered and my appetite gone, I still wanted to belong. So badly.

But I'd messed up.

Again.

The desire to punch the smirks off Sylvia and Emberly's faces pulsed behind my eyes. But I said nothing. Just chewed.

I had failed the test. And she let me.

I wanted to die.

Or rot.

Or reincarnate as a rock—anything but *this*.

They would never accept me now. I'd failed. The bitterness of their judgment stayed lodged in my chest like a stone. They continued talking, completely engrossed in one another, ignoring me entirely. All I could do was nibble at this fucking apple, eyes locked on the splattered pot roast strewn across the hardwood floor.

I grasped for comfort, thinking back to the pictures I used to stare at all day and night just to feel closer to her. Imagining myself as her favorite. She's my everything, this much I know. My eyes began darting side to side, teetering with the idea of letting her know I actually *do* love her. She might already know, but I need to tell her. It can't be so bad right? But Emberly calling me a gluttonous pig? And no one defended me, I understand everyone else, but Syl? I don't know what to think.

***

Everyone had ignored me after dinner. The silent treatment stung, but it was manageable. Tolerable until I could sneak away. As I lay in bed, I kept tossing and turning with no relief. Kept replaying what they'd said. The way they looked at me. I didn't want to think about dinner anymore, but my body wasn't over it. The air in my chest felt tight, like I'd forgotten how to breathe. I had to do something or I was going to scream.

It was one in the morning when the alarm on my phone went off. My heart was beating rapidly when I shoved the covers off. There was something else I needed to get to the bottom of.

It was time.

I needed answers. Now.

I didn't put on my shoes to prevent noise. I stuffed them in my bag with the book included and inched open my door. The hall was quiet, not a sound. As I approached the banister I peered over and noticed the lamp in the living room was on. It was now or never, this could be my only chance. Taking a deep inhale I held my breath and walked on the balls of my feet. Taking each step carefully and to my surprise, the centuries old wood never creaked. As I descended I heard book pages flipping and a slurp of tea. Harriet.

There was no way I could go out the front door without being detected, so I headed to the back through the hall. It wasn't until I opened the door that incessantly squeaked that I said fuck it. I faintly heard Harriet call out, "Hello?"

I made a break for it. Fuck the shoes I needed to get out of there. Shooting down the stairs, I nearly tumbled and definitely acquired splinters as my feet met the asphalt. I heard that distinct squeak again. I didn't have time to cross the lot. My eyes searched for cover and that creepy ass basement came into view. Fuck it. The lock looked broken. Thank God. I managed to shut the door the same time the screen door opened. My heartbeat flooded my ear drums. Harriet didn't say anything that I could hear and figured it would be best to wait a few minutes. There were no windows so the space was pitch black. There could be a serial killer already waiting for me here and I wouldn't be the wiser. I felt around for a lightswitch and came up empty. The space smelled of earth and something metallic. Must be the old ass water heaters down here. It was sharp and a nuisance, but I could handle it a few minutes while I put on my shoes.

I heard the creak of the back door shutting and waited about five minutes until I emerged and headed to the library.

Getting there was no issue, it's a straight shot down from the Flats and about a ten minute walk.

I grabbed at the handle and wiggled an unyielding lock. Damnit. The key cards.

I paced the front, debating on going back and saying I was going for a night run. That was believable right?

Ten minutes passed.

Then—a beep. Two students exited. I darted forward and caught the door just before it closed, ignoring the judgmental glances from inside.

I flashed a hasty smile to the night desk worker and made my way upstairs. Fourth floor. I wasn't sure what I'd find, but Garrett was still missing—and I was still here for a few more days.

Clearly, no one else was doing anything.

And I hadn't seen a single cop since I arrived.

The fourth floor was still empty. I scanned the space before returning to the carrel, hoping I'd missed something the first time.

I checked the shelves. The desks. Nothing.

Finally, I flipped open the strange untitled book again—and there, a few pages in, I found it:

The Doctrine of Discordia by Anonymous. Dated back to the year 1772.

Weird, what would an artifact such as this be left to sit out for public use. Wouldn't that be in an archive somewhere? Doesn't seem like something you would lend out to be abused and used until it breaks.

Flitting through the pages it was unending diagrams to prepare for rituals and I think I saw the word 'chaos' and 'balance' on every other page. Sounds contradictory if you ask me.

I got back to the place I came to and saw only a few margin notes, but nothing that answered any questions. No extra pieces of paper.

I shut the book, defeated. Laying my head on the desktop I shut my eyes and debated falling asleep right here. I was so drained by everything so far, I could pass out from the humiliation at dinner alone. When my eyes cracked back open, I saw it.

Hope came in the form of a bookcase out of place. I could see the hinges on the side. It beckoned me, and I answered the call. Assuming the coast was clear, I grabbed the other side of the case and pulled.

Sure enough, it opened. Beyond was a separate stairwell from the rest. The wooden staircase looked nearly ruined, but still maneuverable. With pressure to check each step down, I eventually made it to the bottom. As I descended I saw no door to each floor, the bottom was the only way out.

I counted five floors instead of four and assume it's the *basement*. Immediately I knew where I was.

The archives.

Parchment maps covered the walls, displaying tunnels snaking beneath campus. Antique books. Yearbooks. Oddities.

And then—I saw it.

Victorian hair art. Made from the hair of the dead, arranged into ornate lace-like patterns. Beautiful, in a way. But deeply unsettling.

A gallery wall full of them stood to my left, under a plaque labeled:

OFFERINGS.

Before I could inspect them, a voice thundered:

"HEY! YOU'RE NOT SUPPOSED TO BE HERE! GET OUT! NOW!"

I froze.

A man stormed toward me, grabbing my arm. Shaking me.

"I—I was just looking for something. I got lost."

He stared hard into my eyes. "Doesn't matter what you're looking for. If you value your place here, you'll stop. It doesn't matter. Now get out."

"Where?" I asked, panicked.

He yanked me toward an elevator—just one button. Ground floor.

He shoved me in.

"Don't get lost here. You'll never be found."

The doors closed.

Only when they opened again and fresh air hit my face did I realize I was shaking.

I ran.

I didn't stop until I reached the Flats.

CHAPTER SEVENTEEN

The next day, Penelope insisted we all head downtown for a Gallery Hop together.

"It's a city staple, Edith," she declared at breakfast. "The streets shut down in the arts district every first Friday of the month. The bars and galleries stay open late. You can't not go."

I sighed, half-impressed by her stamina. "Do you ever grow tired, Penelope? You've got endless energy. I'm envious."

A smile lit up her face as she opened her arm for me to take. "Call me Pen."

***

The day proved to be beautiful, but the hangover was brutal. The sun was breezy, and my head felt like someone had taken a toothbrush to it—clean, but painfully sensitive. Syl tried to persuade me to grab lunch at the student center with her, but I couldn't do it. The greasy food made me nauseous, and the noise only made my headache worse.

When she realized I might throw up, she ditched her food and led me to the cemetery to roll a joint—not even caring that it was a half-mile walk. To be fair, the walk felt good. Being in nature soothed me. It might be the acid I took the other day, but right now, it felt like I was in sync with Syl on a chemical level. Or maybe my mind was just playing tricks on me, offering hope again.

We perched on top of a row of mausoleums embedded in the earth and exhaled the sweet, stinky gift of nature. The bile dropped from my throat, and I felt like I could breathe again. I was sweaty and sticky from all the walking, but my nervous system was finally calming down after last night's chaos. It was stupid. But it was also the best thing ever. The heavens opened and gave me clarity and the rejuvenation I'd been seeking. I didn't need these people—but I wanted them. I wanted Syl, and that was okay.

Since we were close to the Flats and had nothing else to do, Syl suggested we just laze around until the evening. "Trust me, Pen goes crazy when we bar crawl. You'll want to be prepared."

"Heard. I'll probably shower and rest my eyes. I'm pretty stoned right now."

"Okay, I'll come by your room around seven."

Grabbing my bathroom caddy, I took a towel and washcloth from the linen closet. The room had gotten really humid last time, and since there was no vent system, I opened the window to let it air out. The only view was the brick siding of the next flat over—no chance of being seen. I poked my head out to double-check. Below was just a parking lot and the back porch. No windows, no peeping Toms in trees.

The scalding water was a relief for my muscles and mind. I let it beat against my chest, trying to wash away the physical symptoms of anxiety. What they don't tell you about weed is that it actually raises your heart rate. It's not a depressant like alcohol—hence the paranoia and freakouts. I lingered in that gray area of loving the mental fog but hating the way the anxiety crept up just beneath my skin.

I grabbed my shampoo—the one that smelled like Syl's—and closed my eyes, imagining it was her hair I was lathering. Having us together, skin to skin, would definitely make me feel better right now. My chest kept rising and falling, my heart rate accelerating.

I needed to find the right time to talk to her. Privately.

Maybe she was leading me on—so be it. But there was a sliver of hope that she was being genuine and just didn't know how to navigate it. Maybe this was new territory. I was supposed to be her childhood friend, after all.

Since her parents died, she'd grown distant. She couldn't wait to leave for college. My delusions told me our love could conquer anything. That she'd let me be there for her. It stung when Mother offered her a place to stay and she said no. Instead, she isolated herself in that damn house. As a kid, you don't understand why people make the choices they do. Why wouldn't she want sleepovers every night, after having so much stolen from her? When she left at the end of summer, it was supposed to break me—and it did. I was inconsolable. Apparently, it took me months to come out of it and start community college that spring.

I began scrubbing myself ferociously, trying to wash away times I no longer lived in. This was different. We weren't the same people anymore. Maybe she could love me as I am now. Maybe we could get to know each other all over again. I grappled with the idea as I squeezed out the excess water and turned off the faucet.

Stepping onto the bath mat, I heard cars passing on the nearby street and felt the breeze drift in with the steam. I patted my face dry and closed my eyes, silently urging my body to calm down. To breathe.

Then I caught the scent of cigarettes and the sound of voices from the porch below. I crept closer to the window, careful to remain unseen.

I clearly heard Penelope's voice: "I hope it's easier than the first time. I was sick for days after that."

"You really need to compartmentalize better," Emberly replied.

"He was my boyfriend, Em. Have some empathy."

Emberly was matter-of-fact. "I don't have that problem like you. Besides, we made a vow. And considering she's clearly in love with Syl... we'll find out what she's capable of soon enough. She has no choice."

"Yeah, I guess so. Let's head back in—I gotta talk to Harry about a paper due after break."

Oh shit. Shit. What did I just hear? No, no, I didn't just hear that.

I stood frozen, the water on my skin turning ice cold as I broke out in a sweat. Hyperventilating. Trying to stay silent. Trying to make sure they didn't fucking hear me.

The shaking turned to gasping, and the sweat stung

my eyes. I forced myself to calm down enough to shut the window and retreat to my room. The cold house chilled me enough to stave off a full-blown panic attack.

I tried to assess what I knew—and what they knew I knew. They knew I knew about Garrett. But nothing about the book. There's no way they figured out where I went last night... unless they did. I don't know. Shit. What if they had something to do with Garrett? What if I was wrong? What if I'm being delusional again?

There was no way in hell I wanted to be part of them so badly that I'd become an accomplice to a crime for some goddess they chose to worship. There's no way I'd hurt someone—just because I'm in love with Syl.

I had to leave. Fast. And if I could take Syl with me, I would. But I had to protect myself first.

Tiptoeing to my room, I yanked on my clothes, growing exasperated as I struggled to dress over damp skin. I didn't care about anything except finding my keys and getting the fuck out. Forget my stuff—I could buy new things. But I couldn't buy my freedom if I got tied into something like murder.

I searched my bag. Nothing. The nightstand— nothing. Under the bed, in the closet, under the mattress. Nothing. Nothing. Nothing.

I wanted to lock myself in a room and never come out. But that wasn't realistic. I wiped off the sweat and slapped my face a few times. Once I had a grip, I made a plan: act normal. Just say I need something from the car. *Just be cool.*

I took a deep breath and turned the doorknob.

Heading downstairs, I looked in the obvious places

someone might leave their keys, puffing out my cheeks as I meandered through. Emberly and Pen were in the living room as expected, talking to Harriet.

Penelope asked, "Lose something?"

I faked confusion. "Yeah, I'm looking for my car keys. I, uh, left my phone charger in there."

"We have an extra you can use," Emberly offered.

"Well, it's not just that—I was going to grab my meds too. You guys seen my keys anywhere?"

Emberly slid to the side and gestured to the coffee table. "Right here."

That's not where I left them. I *know* it.

I walked into the room, trying not to show how terrified I was, how much I was sweating. I blamed it on the hot shower and the lack of ventilation. Bending down to grab the keys, I backed toward the door.

"Thanks." My hand gripped the knob. So close to freedom.

"I'll be right back."

They watched me. As I backed off the porch, I saw movement in the bay window. I could feel their eyes on me. I didn't look back. I walked slowly, casually. Like I wasn't desperate to escape.

I crossed the street. No footsteps followed. When I reached my car, I got in and immediately locked the doors—

Wait.

I tried once. Twice. A third time. The engine barely sputtered. Then it died.

I popped the hood and looked back—still no one. I stepped out to check the engine, even though I wouldn't know what to do with it. That's when I noticed the tire.

"Not a flat too!"

This is bad. I had no spare. Someone had stolen it a couple years ago.

I didn't even know why I opened the hood. I had no idea what I was doing. I had hardly any money to my name, no way I could afford a car or hotel anywhere.

I'm stuck here.

*****

I stared at the path into the city ahead, unsure why that small gesture tightened something in my chest. I slipped my arm through hers, letting myself sink into the warmth, even if it wouldn't last.

We linked arms, heading into the chill night beneath a sky streaked with midnight purple. The buzz from dinner's wine still hummed faintly in my head.

I told myself I could keep up. I could be a real college kid who goes out late, even with an 8 a.m. class. But as we walked, the faces around us turned into blurs. The lights felt like needles in my eyes.

We passed a couple of dead animals in the road. As we crossed Second Street, Penelope nearly stepped on a flattened rabbit.

"Oh my God—ugh, poor little bunny!" she cried, gripping my arm tighter. "Someone should really clean this shit up!"

"It's just roadkill, Pen. Sentimental about rabbits?"

"Not me." She pulled me closer and lowered her voice. "It's Harriet. Last year Harry took in this cute little bunny named... Curry? No, Curie. Anyway, I feel like shit because my situationship at the time got wasted and, well..."

"What's this have to do with this rabbit?"

"I'm getting there." She took a breath. "He thought Curie was a stuffed animal and threw it into the ceiling fan. It died."

"Ceiling fan? Why the fuck—"

"He was just messing around. You know how boys are. So stupid... I tried to tell Garrett—"

"Garrett?"

"Yeah—anyway, I told him it was shitty and he needed to replace her—"

Before she could continue, Syl body-slammed between us, breaking us apart and cackling.

"Syl! What the fuck!"

"What were you two whispering about?"

"She was telling me about this guy Garrett. How long were you guys together again?" I asked.

"Together?" Syl snorted. "That's pushing it."

"Hey! You shouldn't talk about him like that. He's still missing, you know."

"Oh please, he probably just dropped out. No one even liked him."

Penelope raised her eyebrows, scoffing in disbelief.

I took the opportunity to ask, "What about his car though?"

"Oh come on. He'll be back for it. Probably just using it as long-term parking."

"You know," Penelope mused, "that does sound like him."

"It does, because it is," Syl concluded, tapping our

shoulders before rejoining Harriet and Emberly.

Penelope resumed our hushed conversation. "I know I can seem like a bitch, but seriously—Syl's the mean girl of the group. I don't know what she was like when you two were friends, but sometimes she just cuts deep."

Were friends. That stung like hell.

"I don't know. I feel like all teenagers are angsty."

"Touché." Penelope flipped her hair. "For what it's worth, no one ever passes that test. I didn't think they'd throw your plate against a wall, but I think you're all good now.

"Here though? We're never the guest of honor. That's reserved."

"For who?"

"Our goddess. Discordia!" she squealed, then immediately looked back to make sure no one overheard. "I know it sounds weird—rigorous and all—but it's real. Like, *really* real."

Pen leaned in, whispering directly into my ear, "But the rewards are far greater than you can imagine when you're one of us. I did something I thought I could never do. But now, I'm rich—and I have my whole life laid out for me."

Pulling away, she stared ahead, farther than any of us could see. "I have big plans, Ed. And it's all thanks to her."

I didn't know what to say, so I huffed a hollow laugh and kept putting one foot in front of the other.

We continued weaving down the sidewalks, jaywalking whenever possible. The streets were nearly empty by 10 p.m. The Art Hop stretched from Fourth to Eighth Street. It felt like miles. But Pen knew the way—

she'd been to every bar crawl and art event in town. She reveled in pointing out grim little sights: the dead crow off Church Street, a fat rat couple by a sewer grate. When we passed the flattened remains of a dog, her groan sounded almost genuine.

She whined through the last few blocks. "I need a fucking drink! How much farther?"

"Pen, you *know* how much farther," Emberly replied, bored.

Pen tossed her head back dramatically. "I'm *trying* to be cute here. Don't be a cunt—just go with it."

Emberly's expression went flat. "Whining's never cute. And neither is calling me a cunt."

"Whatever," Pen muttered, rolling her eyes. She clamped her arm tighter around mine, quickening her pace as she dragged me along. She aimed us straight for an Irish pub on Fourth St., parting the sea of people like a blade. She called a man over 250 pounds a bitch as she wedged through the door, leaving me slightly stunned. I couldn't imagine moving through a space so boldly. She wasn't afraid to take up space; she demanded everyone accept her presence. And I was in awe.

That's when I saw the bulletin board where people posted business cards and flyers. A face caught my eye. I didn't recognize him at first, but then I saw the black, all-caps sans-serif: MISSING – GARRETT SMITH followed by details I couldn't read from where I stood. Hearing the rumors around campus was one thing; seeing his face physically posted like that sent a pit through my stomach. The flyer was half-torn and wrinkled, fluttering in the draft from the entrance.

Penelope kept dragging us through the crowd as if nothing mattered except reaching the bar. She was laser-focused, huddling into the space and ordering a round before Emberly even got to the counter. I half-expected to feel out of place, but her energy was magnetic.

Bad bluegrass warbled through the speakers. Laughter and voices wrapped around me like an overused quilt. It wasn't my style—but I hadn't felt this alive in ages.

The bartender handed me a Guinness, and I waited a full minute before taking a sip, savoring the malty bitterness. As I turned to take in the room, the drunken come-ons and lingering stares hit me like static. All I saw were tired, blank faces—men running from their demons, women wrapped in the cloak of alcohol. It was stifling and humid, like the bar was breathing me in and exhaling hot, sticky air. I held my breath, trying not to let the overwhelming heat get to me.

It took forever to reach the bar counter, but only seconds to make my way back outside. The street was foggier than I remembered. The ground felt like sand under my feet, my thoughts sinking and rising, moving in cycles like waves, threatening to sweep me under. No one came to check on me. That familiar bitterness grew in my throat, almost choking me. After everything, Sylvia was still at the center of everything, as if she owned my attention without ever earning it. Why did she push herself on me only to leave me feeling discarded?

This is nothing to me, I told myself.

I pushed my way back through the door, straightened my posture, and tilted my chin up, ignoring the grime on my shoes. I scanned the bar and saw Sylvia—flushed and laughing—throwing herself into Emberly's arms, murmuring something I couldn't hear.

All the intrusive thoughts sank like a stone in my stomach. I was right there. But I felt like a stranger.

Sylvia was right there, close enough to touch. And yet—she just slipped away.

Penelope was already on her second drink when I returned. Without warning, she grabbed my wrist, spun me around, and planted a kiss on my lips.

To my own surprise, I kissed her back.

Her lips were soft. The moment felt like a surreal bubble of relief—a pause from everything weighing me down. A kiss wasn't what I *wanted*, but it was... something.

We pulled away laughing. "Hey, you started it!" Pen said, grinning. "I was just finishing it."

I felt Sylvia's eyes on me. A flash of something—jealousy? Anger?

I tried to act like I didn't care. But watching her react—watching her *feel* something—made my heart skip.

The breeze outside revived Penelope. She skipped ahead, shouting, "Off to the next one, bitches!"

Harriet lingered behind, her eyes far away. I offered her my arm. I could tell she wasn't eager to catch up.

"The world without humans is so peaceful," she murmured, glancing at the empty street. "Yet here I am."

I nodded, understanding more than I could explain. It always felt like we were both drifting at the edges, pulled along by others' momentum.

I lost count after the second bar. Then the third. Then the fourth.

I'd taken birthday shots with strangers. Swapped beer

for wine.

One bar had a tequila shot special. Penelope raised her glass: "After tonight, you're *ours*, Ed—and we're not letting you go! To never falling from grace! Cheers, you cunts!"

I prayed to whatever goddess they believed in that no one saw my hand tremble as I raised my shot and downed it. As if that gesture sealed the deal. I didn't want to be, but a bigger part of me was bubbling with excitement. I surpassed my expectations.

Syl leaned over to speak in my ear over the blaring shitty live band, "Congratulations Edie."

This was totally unlike me, and I was *not* well. Penelope and Emberly were drinking machines, carrying on with composure I could only envy. Emberly had a kind of drunk stoicism; she never missed a beat, still scanning the room like she'd remember every detail the following day. Sylvia was glued to her hip, elbowing her way through the crowd to keep drinks coming, glowing with that signature, rosy, alcohol-induced flush.

Penelope was in her element, shrieking across the room, commanding every guy's attention. Soon, they pulled us into their VIP booth, tossing back shots like royalty.

Pen dove into a chugging contest, arms flung wide like the whole world belonged to her.

Harriet stayed quiet, ghostlike, watching it all. She moved with an unsettling calm, repelling attention without trying. Guys avoided her without knowing why.

And me? I rode the wave. Euphoric. Slightly nauseated. At one point I ran to an alley and spat bile behind a dumpster.

This wasn't my kind of night. Not small-town bars where everyone knew each other either. This was an eclectic nightmare.

Girls in matching black leotards and mom jeans. Hair in beachy waves. Clone faces.

Finance bros with breath like whiskey and bravado, whispering oily compliments into ears that didn't ask.

It was perfect. Awful. Hilarious. A mess that matched mine.

For once, I was okay with the nausea in my gut. With the wreckage around me.

Compared to these people, I felt superior.

Pretentious, maybe. But I wasn't hiding it.

I didn't live for weekends. I was something else. A strategist. A piece moving others on a board.

In some opera-themed trash bar, I caught sight of my reflection in the ornate mirror behind the bar. I looked up to make sure I didn't look pale and sickly. Instead I *had* an inkling to look up, so I did. And I saw myself, standing in the back, smirking and standstill. Watching. Waiting.

When I turned around, of course I saw nothing. I tried to stop it, but now, I was really going to get sick. I had to get some fresh air.

Putting a hand on the brick wall I felt my way down the alley. Listening to the buzz and ringing in my ears drown out the sounds of the crowds I tried not to see my last meal again when I heard, "Hey!"

Through my teary eyes, I saw Syl running toward me. "You okay?"

"Yeah. Just trying to keep my shit together."

She laid a hand on my back, rubbing slow circles. "Start humming," she said gently.

It helped. The nausea passed.

I thanked her and leaned back against the brick, watching my breath fog up the night.

I couldn't stop staring at her—her knee-high stockings, thick eyeliner, tipsy grace.

In my drunken haze, I asked, "Do you ever think about how different things would be if you stayed?"

She kept watching the groups at the end of the alley. "Stayed where?"

Seriously? "Home."

She didn't blink. Took a few steady breaths. Then laughed lightly.

"Oh God. No."

When her eyes met mine, I felt exposed. She could see the sweat on my forehead.

"What would I even be doing?" she asked. "Working at some depressing diner? Dating some loser from high school?" She shook her head, smiling like it was absurd.

I wanted to throw up again. But I swallowed it.

"What if we…" I started.

Not the nausea this time—just the confession lodged in my throat.

Rolling her eyes, Syl groaned. "What if what?"

She needed to know. We could leave. Start over.

Screw this place.

Screw *them*.

We could find something better. Together.

"Spit it out, Edie. What if we what?"

I looked at her, really looked—not only to debate

ending my question, but to let myself imagine it. "…had dated."

For a second, she looked disoriented. Like the thought had never occurred to her. All I could picture was her hand in mine. A different life. A better one.

Instead she looked like I'd just ruined her night.

Was it disgust? At the question? At *me*?

I shoved it down.

"Forget it. I think I'm good now, let's get back to everyone," brushing off and adjusting my clothes I gestured for her to lead the way.

Then, like nothing happened, she gives me the same perfect, photo-ready smile she's given a hundred times before. Her fingers slip around my wrist, tugging me back toward the bar. Like I imagined everything.

After a few more stops, we found ourselves at a rooftop bar, neon lights flashing around us like a dystopian rave. Pen was at home here, draped over the railing as she gestured wildly toward a hotel a few blocks over, where we could just make out the glow of a rooftop pool. "Look!" she shouted, pointing. "They're hooking up *right there*, on the deck!"

We all leaned over, straining to see the blurry figures moving in the distance.

I smirked. "Someone's got a kink for being watched."

"Ya think?" Harriet replied with a raised brow, and Sylvia giggled, and I could feel the vomit coming up in my throat, wondering who had seen *her* naked.

Emberly's gaze was fixed on the scene. "There's a thrill in doing something where you *might* get caught, but when they are… they freeze."

Sylvia nodded, eyes glazed, like her thoughts were somewhere far away.

I downed another shot, watching her.

That hollow look. That weight behind her silence.

It gnawed at me.

What are you hiding, Syl?

Chapter Eighteen

Not long after our final stop, Penelope couldn't keep anything down—not even water. Twenty-five minutes later, her throat sounded like sandpaper. Syl was the unlucky one holding back her hair, and Penelope latched onto her neck, vomit still on her breath.

"Syl! Carry me! I love you so much. Are you still my friend?"

"Of course, Pen," Sylvia said indifferently, as if this were routine.

"I'd kill for you, bitch."

"I know, Pen. I love you, too."

Penelope's voice softened to a whisper. "You're the only one I feel safe around. Make sure I get home."

We managed to drag her limp body to First Street before she suddenly sprang back to life. Out of nowhere, she was upright, bolting down the sidewalk like someone had injected her with pure adrenaline.

She zigzagged across the pavement, veering left, then right, leading us toward a small grassy patch beside the highway. She finally collapsed into the grass and pulled a small box from her pocket. I watched as she took out what looked like a cigarette, stuffed it with some ground-up flower from the box, and lit the end.

Penelope exhaled and held it out like an offering. "I don't feel so sick now."

She tried to pass it to Emberly, who was already rolling her own.

"No way I'm smoking that after you just puked."

"Hey, not my fault. And I rinsed with water," Pen pouted, shrugging off Emberly's glare. "More for me."

I glanced around and realized we were near the campus cemetery. This little field felt hidden from the world—no streetlights, no houses, just a forgotten patch of earth beside the highway.

"What is this place?" I asked, hoping someone knew.

"It's state-owned. Penelope works with the historic district and comes here to smoke all the time."

The setting was beautiful—the hum of the highway in the distance, the skyline glowing softly in the background. Even the isolation felt safe, like we were sealed away in a pocket of quiet that belonged only to us.

They all laughed as Penelope took another drag, but her eyelids were already starting to droop. A glance at Sylvia told me she noticed too, but she only tossed a shoulder, leaning back on her elbows, relaxed and unconcerned.

Then Penelope's eyes closed completely. I looked at Harriet. "What do we do?"

Harriet sighed. "She's fine. Just leave her. As Em said, at least she's on her side this time."

I knelt beside her, watching for the rise and fall of her chest. When I was sure she was breathing, I slipped the box from her hand and tucked it into my pocket. I might need a little more for myself later. She wouldn't miss it.

The earthy, smoky scent lingered in my lungs, calming me. Right here, in the middle of nowhere, with people who—for now—seemed genuine, I felt almost comforted.

The familiar haze of an indica hybrid was exactly what I'd been missing. As I exhaled, the city lights softened and shimmered, flickering in and out of focus like a dream. Everything—the buildings, the traffic, the smog—seemed distant and hyperreal, each detail sharp and surreal.

Emberly and Harriet talked about classes and bizarre theories, while Sylvia sat silently, her gaze fixed on something far away. The conversation dissolved into background noise, abstract and unimportant. I didn't have to speak, and I was grateful for the stillness.

Eventually, Emberly began pointing out constellations and spinning myths from thin air. The others leaned in, wide-eyed, hanging on every word.

Sylvia talked about a project she had for class—some vague obstacle she'd "overcome." I almost rolled my eyes. Classic Sylvia. Making the mundane sound like a fucking odyssey. But I kept my mouth shut, letting it pass through me like fog.

Then Emberly's voice cut through the haze. "Hey, Edith! Don't hog it!"

I blinked, realizing I'd zoned out. The joint was burning low between my fingers. I handed it off quickly, feeling my cheeks flush. The joint continued its lazy orbit, and our conversation slid into something quieter: art, light pollution, the mysteries above our heads.

Eventually it reached the filter, and we all sat in the shared silence, still drifting in our own worlds.

I didn't know these women well—not even Syl, I was starting to realize. But in that eerie quiet, I felt strangely tethered to them.

There was peace here, in this odd little corner of the world. Then the fucking bell chime went off again, breaking the stillness. I couldn't help it—I checked the time. To my surprise, it was actually on the hour. *Finally,* I thought, *it got it right once.* Now I could die in peace.

After a while, we turned to look at Penelope, flat on her back.

"She's still out," Harriet observed, calm as ever.

Emberly stretched, eyes scanning the horizon. "Guess we'd better get her back. Ed, grab her arms. Harriet, take the legs. I'll grab the middle."

I nodded and moved into position. Lifting her was awkward and heavy, but somehow, we managed it. We shuffled forward slowly, muscles burning, sweat beading on my forehead. No one said a word.

When Sylvia needed a break, we set Penelope down on the hill's slope. I bent over, catching my breath, hands on my knees.

That's when I noticed Penelope's eyelids flutter. She gave me a crooked, sleepy grin and let out a chuckle.

I was about to crack a joke about her sudden revival when the ground tilted, my vision went black, and I was knocked to the ground by an unseen force. Hard.

***

My vision was a total blur as I came to, but I vividly felt

the ache and massive knot on the back of my head as it bounced against someone's chest.

I was being carried.

My limbs felt like cement.

Through blinking, watery vision, I made out Harriet's calm expression. Emberly leaned in over me.

"She's waking up."

I should have felt relieved. But their faces weren't filled with concern.

They looked... pleased.

Unsettlingly pleased.

Without warning, they dropped me. I hit the ground hard. Pain rang through my entire body.

And then—

Sylvia brought a branch crashing down across my head.

And darkness took me again.

Chapter Nineteen

I blinked, my vision swimming as the dark shape of the floor slowly came into focus beneath me. My wrists burned where the rope bit into my skin, binding my arms tightly behind me. I tried shifting my legs, but they were bound to the chair—solid, unmovable, like steel. Pain pulsed through my skull in waves, a dull, relentless drumbeat echoing inside my head.

A single flickering light swayed above me, casting warped shadows that dissolved into pitch black at the basement's edges. The air was cold and damp, laced with the metallic scent of rust and earth. I squinted into the dark until something moved—a figure stepping into the light, her face smooth and incomprehensible her eyes colder than steel.

Emberly.

She leaned casually against the cinder block wall, arms crossed, just... watching me, like she was waiting for a punchline.

"What do you want?" My voice came out hoarse, scraped raw on its way up my throat.

Emberly tilted her head, eyes dragging over me with

the detached curiosity of someone studying a pinned butterfly. "That's on a need-to-know basis."

Her calm, clinical tone sent a chill prickling up my spine.

"This has to be a joke. Some twisted prank thing you all cooked up in a drunken haze?"

She didn't answer. She just stared. A faint, infuriating smile pulling at the corner of her mouth.

"What's got you, Ed?" Her voice was smooth, but there was something sharp beneath it. Something dark. Something I should've seen coming.

My face flushed with anger. I twisted against the ropes, the fibers slicing deeper into my wrists. "Any sane person would be panicking right now—tied up like this."

"All the better for us," she said, stepping closer. "Oh, sweetheart... I've been tying people up for a long time in much tighter knots. So go ahead—struggle all you want. It's cute."

"Maybe they were amateurs."

She shrugged. "Maybe."

"So this is a hazing ritual, then?"

"I guess you could say that." Her tone was flat, almost bored. The shadows deepened across her face as her smile twisted into something meaner.

The fear crept in like rising water. I tried to keep my voice steady. "What's your problem, anyway?"

She raised a brow. "I think we both know it's *you*."

"Me?" I scoffed, even as my pulse thundered in my ears. "I haven't done anything to any of you."

I was gearing up to snap back when her fist slammed into my jaw.

Stars exploded across my vision. The chair tipped, crashing to the floor. My head hit hard, jolting everything sideways. Through the ringing in my ears, I barely registered her hands gripping the back of the chair and hauling me upright like I weighed nothing. Like I was a doll she was repositioning.

She leaned in close, her voice curling like smoke. "You should've never come here, Edith."

Up close, her grin stretched too wide, too fake. She lifted her hand, and a flash of metal caught the light.

A blade.

She pressed it to my throat—cold, sharp, unforgiving.

My pulse surged beneath its edge. A scream tried to claw its way out, but I swallowed it.

The knife pressed harder, just enough to whisper pain into my skin. Her eyes studied my face, hungry for the fear crawling across it. Her gaze gleamed with something I couldn't name but instantly recognized.

"Not much of a fighter, are you?" Her teeth gleamed as she smiled, fingers brushing my collarbone before lifting the blade away. "Such a shame."

My skin went cold. She wasn't bluffing. She was *enjoying* this. Every second. Every flinch.

Above us, faint voices drifted through the floorboards—laughter, maybe Penelope's distinctive snort. Emberly slipped the knife back into her pocket and stepped away with the same casual air as someone waiting on a bus.

She vanished into the shadows just as I heard footsteps moving across the floor above, the boards creaking and groaning under their weight. My pulse throbbed, the blood pounding in my ears as I strained to listen, half-expecting a fresh wave of pain to descend. Instead, the voices grew louder, feet shuffling, getting closer.

I thrashed against the ropes, desperation flaring like an electric shock. "Help! Fire! Someone—"

Footsteps thundered on the stairs. My voice died as the basement door creaked open, and a shadowy figure stepped through. Then another, and another. They filed in, their faces hidden in the dark, but I could feel their eyes on me, cold and unblinking.

The light flickered, catching Penelope's smug smile, Emberly's sharp stare, and Sylvia's blank expression.

She held my gaze. Steady. Unflinching. More damning than all the others.

I slumped in the chair, my voice barely a whisper. "I'm not going anywhere, am I?"

Sylvia stepped forward, her expression hardening.

"No, Edith. You're not."

CHAPTER TWENTY

Before

Graduation felt surreal. My mind spun with the lights, the caps flung into the air—but I kept glancing at Syl, who was already looking my way. In that moment, I knew—whether forever or not, our connection was real. Unbreakable. Or at least, it felt that way.

I watched her in the midday heat, her hair frizzing beneath her graduation cap, and thought: This was supposed to be our adventure. We were meant to see what lay beyond these walls, our paths woven together. I'd follow her anywhere. Didn't she understand we were forever?

Those nights we spent together, I'd lie in bed pretending to sleep until she drifted off first. Then, unable to resist, I'd turn toward her, staring at the back of her head, inhaling the faint scent of Pantene in her hair. I'd match her breathing, clinging to that moment like a secret I could keep. Her breath beside me lulled me into a restless kind of peace. I'd watch her face, traced in silver light, feeling close to her in a way words could never describe. One night, unable to help myself, I leaned closer, close enough that my nose touched her exposed neck. The moonlight fell softly on her skin, the silk pajamas hugging her form. She looked so beautiful, and it took every ounce of control not to press my lips against her neck to mark that part of her as my own. The fantasy that she might one day turn around, her eyes meeting mine, wasn't just a thought—it was a need. And in that silence, I felt like a vampire waiting for dawn, my desire consuming me from the inside out.

But she would never feel the same. I tried to ignore the sinking feeling in my gut, the question that wouldn't stop: Will she ever see me as more?

Hope isn't a plan, I told myself one night, standing in the bathroom, my face blurred in the mirror by scalding steam. How can I look like this, feel so much, and still not be what she wants?

My face burned—red and swollen from the water and from crying. My reflection stared back, unfamiliar. Syl brought out the worst in me—the needy, the desperate, the small. I didn't want to be that person, but I couldn't stop. She was the one who'd always been there, the one who made me feel whole. But how much of myself would I lose before I admitted it was one-sided?

***

I never told Syl about those times when I'd steal small things of hers, those pieces of her she'd leave behind. Once, I even pulled a strand of hair from her brush and pressed it between rose petals, hiding it under my bed. I'd hold it in my hand, imagining these fragments might bring me closer to her.

Then I started reading about magic. Spells. The fascination turned dark and thrilling until I found a ritual—love spells, the page said. One line stood out: "Through blood, a bond."

It was like a light flicked on in the darkest part of my mind.

One morning, Syl left a used tampon in the bathroom bin. I took it, squeezing the blood into a jar, mixing it with her hair and honey. The thick red stained my fingers. I felt closer to her than ever as I smeared the excess across my face. For a moment, I felt powerful—like I held something sacred, something real. That jar held a piece of her soul, something she'd never give me freely. There was nothing else in the world I wanted more.

As I began preparing the ritual, Syl walked in. She froze. Her eyes locked on me, on the jar in my hands, the blood on my face.

"What the hell are you doing?"

I couldn't come up with a lie. My mind raced, but my heart pounded louder than thought. "Syl—"

"Is that… is that my tampon? Edith, what the actual—"

Her voice sharpened, cracking into panic. "No. You know what? I'm leaving. This… this is insane."

"Wait!" I grabbed her wrist, pulling her back toward me.

She looked deeply into me, her face a mix of horror and something I couldn't place. I let go, letting her retreat to the door, but something inside me snapped. I knew this was the last chance to say what I'd hidden and prayed for in dreams. "Syl, I love you."

She laughed, hollow and stunned, her face twisted with revulsion. "What? You think this is love?"

"But it is. It's always been love," I said, desperate for her to see. "It's only ever been you."

"Edith, you don't know what love is," she said, voice like ice. "You're not my friend. You're—this is sick. How long have you been like this?"

Something broke in me. I don't know what happened next— only that I grabbed the ceramic kettle from my desk and swung. Not to kill. Just to make her stop.

Her body crumpled. Her head hit the carpet with a dull thud. I stood over her, panting, watching the rise and fall of her chest. The slow, steady pulse in her throat. No blood, but knocked unconscious

just enough to not break her skull.
    I hope she doesn't remember this.

Chapter Twenty-One

I had no idea how long I'd been down here. My thumb throbbed from where I'd broken it to slip the binding. The rope hung slack around my wrist, but escape was still impossible. Like clockwork, I heard footsteps creaking on the stairs—no way to hide what I'd done.

I never imagined they'd be capable of real torture. That was my first mistake. These women weren't the people I presume. They were shadows—hard edges of every dark impulse in Sylvia's mind, the softness gone. I knew they wanted something, but I still didn't know what. The interrogations dragged on endlessly, and the question never changed:

"Do you know why you're here?"

My answer never changed either. *I have no fucking idea what you're talking about!* I'd scream it, shout it, hoping one of them would finally crack, take pity, and let me go.

But they never did. At least one of them was always on watch, even when I couldn't see her. I could hear the cigarette drags from outside the door, waiting for a whimper or a cry—something they could use to justify keeping me here.

Once, I asked Sylvia, *"If I answer, will you let me go? Aren't you afraid I'll tell the police?"*

She crouched down in front of me, her face too close, unblinking.

"Oh, Edith," she whispered, almost tender. "Only by telling the truth will you earn the right to decide when death becomes you. The longer you lie, the more you suffer. Be honest, and death will be swift. You're never leaving this place."

She didn't even wait for a reply—just stood and walked out.

I'm dying, I thought, slumped and bound.

But then I reminded myself: *I'm not dead yet.*

I forced myself upright, my spine aching from how long I'd been in the same position. My muscles were stiff, almost useless. Sylvia thought I'd rot in this corner, that I'd give up. They all did. But what they didn't see—what none of them saw—was that people who thought they were invincible were always the easiest to break. One of my eyes was swollen shut. Emberly had taken to prodding it with her fingers, like she was tending a bruise just to see it bloom. I'd stopped reacting—no screams, just flinches and glares—but it was enough for her. She got off on it. Pretending to be in charge, even when Penelope was the one doing the talking, circling me like a vulture, dragging her paring knife across the cinder block wall.

She liked to watch—I could tell. The way she strutted, glancing at me like a kid about to rip the arms off a doll. Then the blade would press into my back, just an inch deep, but sharp enough to steal my breath. I didn't scream anymore. She pulled it out, twisting it in her palm.

"It's like cutting into cheese," she said. "All those crime shows? I thought they were exaggerating."

I waited for Sylvia to stop her. But she was a phantom—only appearing when the others weren't around. I'd lost track of time. Days? Weeks? I couldn't remember the last time I drank real water, just the drips from a leaking pipe. I was so dehydrated that time blurred, smeared into delirium. They force-fed me slop—some kind of blended mush, more vomit than food. I kept just enough down to stay alive.

In those rare moments of quiet, I tried to think. They had to take shifts. I figured that out by the way footsteps faded, then changed. Like they were keeping each other entertained. I memorized the rhythm, waiting for that one crack in the pattern—my chance.

I thought of all the ways I'd come back to haunt them. I pictured their faces, smug and self-righteous, breaking down into panic and horror. I'd have them begging to confess, pleading for a way out. I clung to the image like it was the only thing keeping me breathing. This wouldn't last forever. I could feel it like something old and familiar in my gut.

***

One day, Penelope cooed from the dark, "You'll admit what you did, and it'll all be over." The blade twisted in her hand again, hovering over the same spot. But I could see in her eyes that she was almost bored, ready to move on to something sharper, harder to endure.

***

I counted footsteps in every hour, every pattern. The fucking bell chime at the church couldn't be trusted with giving an accurate chime on the hour, however, I knew it was around three in the afternoon when Harriet was coming down because she was the only punctual one for her shift. I heard the slide, the scuff of her shoes against the floor.

If she wore white, she'd look like a ghost—pale face, eyes too wide, always drifting like she wasn't really there. I didn't flinch when she stepped into the light.

"You like acupuncture?" she asked, as if she was recommending a drink.

"You offering?" I rasped, lips cracked, sarcasm thin but intact.

She arched a brow, reached into her pocket, and pulled out a needle.

"Hold still."

It wasn't pain exactly—it was worse. An itch under the skin, a pulsing need to claw at the pressure points she hit, every placement deliberate, surgical.

"Why are you helping me?" I managed to ask one night, half-dazed.

"I'm sticking needles in your skin," she muttered, not looking up.

"Fair enough."

It was the worst kind of torture—small enough to endure, sharp enough to drive me mad. But even that wouldn't break me. I told myself it was practice, something to keep me sharp for the moment I'd need to be more demanding, more robust.

***

The basement would fall silent in short spurts, and I'd be left alone with my thoughts, planning through the fog of exhaustion. Every time I nodded off, they'd rouse me—water in the face, a tap from a boot, laughing as if my suffering was their favorite pastime. Harriet kept running little experiments on me, testing pressure points, scraping my skin for samples until I felt like a dummy for their sick pleasure. Emberly's face would come close sometimes, leaning in, her breath hot against my skin, like she could smell the defeat they hoped I'd feel. But I kept thinking of Sylvia.

I saw her face in every possibility, even twisted in contempt. I held on to the version of her that once existed, if only to remember what betrayal looked like. I wouldn't let her win. I wouldn't let *any* of them win.

So whenever I was alone, I ran the plan again and again. I clung to every flicker of strategy, every flash of hope. A stray piece of rebar barely noticeable sat in the corner, it was so close, soon it would be in my grasp. I wouldn't be here forever. I could feel it building—adrenaline rising like a storm, waiting for a single mistake.

It only takes one.

Chapter Twenty-Two

"Are you afraid?" Harriet's voice sliced through the dark, casual but laced with menace. She leaned in, her pale hair catching what little light there was—the only detail not swallowed by the shadows.

"Define afraid," I muttered, my throat raw from dehydration and too much screaming.

She hummed, studying me like a pinned insect under glass. Then, without a word, she straightened, pivoted, and vanished into the black. Her footsteps faded, leaving behind a silence so thick it pressed on my chest. Alone again—a brief, bitter mercy in this hellhole.

I couldn't wait any longer. My heart pounded as I held my breath, listening. Harriet moved through the kitchen, down the hall, into the living room. The soft groan of wood, the shift of fabric—she'd settled into her reading nook. I counted five agonizing minutes. Now or never.

Gritting my teeth, I flung my weight backward. The chair legs cracked, the frame splintering with a loud snap. Pain exploded through my back and shoulders as I hit the ground, but adrenaline drowned it out. I was alive. Above, footsteps thundered across the floor. I had seconds.

My hands were still tied. The rough cords cut into my skin, but I twisted, feeling the ropes slacken. The dampness from the leaking pipe above had tightened the knots a bit. I pulled, my double-jointed elbow straining as I bent my shoulder in a way that shouldn't have been possible. With a final wrenching twist, the rope gave way, and my hands fell free.

A laugh escaped me—a mixture of relief and disbelief. I'd actually done it. The door upstairs crashed open, and I knew I had little time. Panic surged as I clawed at the rope binding my legs, fingers slipping on the damp, fraying strands.

"Get it together," I hissed, forcing myself to focus. The footsteps above grew heavier, closer. The air thickened—humid, suffocating—the walls pressing inward. Every nerve screamed at me to move, but my legs were still bound. The last knot came loose just as shadows spilled across the stairwell. I launched forward, instinct overriding thought, my heart hammering against my ribs.

Pain shot through my side—Emberly's bruises still fresh—but I buried it, eyes fixed on the door.

"What the—she can't be loose!" a voice snarled from above.

I didn't look back.

My vision swam. My breath tore out in ragged gasps, each one syncing with the pounding footsteps behind me. The concrete floor was cold, punishing, bruising my bare feet with every step. The room tilted. My body dragged behind my mind, which screamed only one word: *Run*.

The last few feet stretched out for what felt like miles.

My head throbbed, vision blurring at the edges, but I kept going. The rebar sat in the distant corner. I could have grabbed it, but there wasn't enough time, I had to get the fuck out of here. I knew when I saw sunlight I was out of the basement, my body numb to the pain, my mind locked onto one thought: *freedom*. Even as the light outside seemed impossibly far, I pushed forward, knowing I would die trying if it meant I didn't die here, in this place, in their hands.

Chapter Twenty-Three

There were no words when they blocked my path outside the basement. Just kicking. My bones screamed as they beat me down again and again. They didn't stop until they were too tired to keep going. I was already broken, but now even the ropes binding my hands felt pointless.

I tried to push myself up—one arm bracing, the other useless. Penelope kicked my elbow. Blood sprayed from my mouth. My teeth rattled in their sockets. One more kick and they'd come loose, tumbling from my gums like dice.

I spit blood. Tried to breathe, even as my ribs throbbed—cracked, maybe broken. The only sound was the slow drip of water from the pipe above, tapping against my scalp. Drip, drip, drip. It made me wonder if death might actually be a relief.

I don't know when I gave up. Maybe it was when Penelope laughed. Or when my legs twisted beneath me, tangled in the chair that wouldn't stop tipping over. I wasn't some fantasy heroine summoning strength at the last second. I was just tired.

Still, some stubborn part of me hoped. If my body

couldn't move, maybe my mind still could. Maybe someone was coming. Maybe I could make it out.

But I knew better.

Penelope's final kick snapped my head to the side. She smiled sweetly. "God, I didn't think I'd miss this—but I *do*."

I didn't bother begging. Sympathy was a dead end. I stretched one arm toward the door—pathetic, desperate.

Then Emberly stepped on my forearm.

I yelped, shoved at her with my free hand, but she didn't move. "It's like fighting a toddler," she said, grinning.

Her weight shifted. Then the snap.

Pain shot through me—white, electric, numbing. I screamed. My arm bent at a sickening angle, bone pressing against skin. Emberly just sneered.

"Pathetic," she muttered, spitting on me before walking away.

I rolled to my side, staring at the flickering light above. I let myself cry. No one cared. They'd watched me be tortured for days—weeks?—and no one flinched anymore.

"Why?" I croaked, voice dry and broken.

Syl stepped forward. Her boots clicked on the floor—deliberate, menacing. Hands clasped behind her back, head tilted like she was examining something in a museum.

"Because you're a murderer, Edith Aldridge," she said.

Her words cut deeper than their kicks.

Before I could answer, she gestured. Penelope and

Harriet dragged me up, their fingers digging into my bruised flesh. I didn't fight. What would be the point? Emberly tossed a rope over the pipe, and they tied my hands high above my head.

Pain ignited in my shattered arm—lightning through my shoulder. My toes barely brushed the ground. My legs were still tangled in the broken chair. When the crying stopped, Syl was there, inches from my face, lips curled into a grin.

"I know who you are now," I whispered.

"What?" she snapped.

"You're just a Bunny."

She rolled her eyes. Then kneed me between the legs. The pain was blinding.

"I wouldn't be cracking jokes if I were you," she hissed. "You're about to die, Edith. Don't you get that?"

"What's stopping you? I'm right here," I said. The words slipped out before I could stop them.

Syl laughed—sharp, hollow. "Because I want you to suffer first. Like my parents did. And I'm going to record your confession."

"That would be a lie," I muttered.

Her face twisted. Then she was screaming—raw and guttural, a sound that tore through me.

"YOU FUCKING MURDERER! YOU KILLED MY PARENTS!"

She yanked the rope, jerking my arms higher. Pain exploded through my broken limb, and I screamed. She didn't stop. She ranted—breathless, furious, every sentence a weapon.

I tried to block her out. Tried to disappear into my

mind. But then she grabbed a knife—Emberly's—and pointed it at me.

"Admit it," she growled. "Admit what you did."

I whispered, "I didn't do anything. I just went to the library and—"

She stabbed me.

Once. Twice. Three times.

"No. You were trying to get ahead of us. Like always. You were going to kill us before we killed you."

The blade sank into my legs. Pain surged, white-hot and unbearable. Then into my arm—my bicep useless now, torn open. Blood poured out, warm and slick, pooling beneath me.

Syl stood over me, chest heaving, eyes dark and empty. She didn't say another word.

I couldn't hold on anymore. My vision blurred. My body floated, distant and heavy. I wanted to be anywhere else.

Syl turned to the others. "Stitch her up. Clean her up. Don't leave her alone."

Then she was gone—footsteps fading upstairs.

Harriet grabbed her kit. Penelope sighed as I sank deeper into myself, barely hearing their voices through the static in my mind.

Somewhere, deep inside, a spark still flickered.

I wasn't dead yet.

I still had to find a way out if I wanted to live. I wasn't a hero. But I could be something else.

I just had to survive long enough to become it.

CHAPTER TWENTY-FOUR

Before: Sylvia

This morning, I woke to a silence so deep it felt like the earth had swallowed itself. My ears rang with a high, deafening pitch that blurred everything. But last night? Last night was still crystal clear.

I texted Stephen—the boy toy I keep on hand to take the edge off. He'll do anything for a chance to get laid, always willing to play boyfriend if there's something in it for him. He's sweet, pliable, and naive. Easy to keep in a box and pull out when I need a kind of love I can't ask for. It's always the same: flash doe eyes, part your lips just right, and they'll do anything. I craved attention. They craved whatever I'd give freely—but only after they played my game.

I'd never tell Edie, of course. She's my best friend, but anytime I mention hooking up with guys, she gets pissed. She doesn't get it. Hell, sometimes I think no one does. I've never felt more alone. When I was younger, Dad would take me fishing or out for nine holes whenever I felt like this. It used to help. Not anymore.

Back when teenage boys thought cruelty was love, I had nights I couldn't even cry myself to sleep. Dad always heard me. The creak of the floorboards was enough.

He'd find me in the bathroom, blowing my nose, and pull me into his chest—half-asleep, beer belly between us. "Let's go for a drive," he'd mumble. Code for: grab your clubs and let's go hit balls into the woods.

Golf was his way of speaking to a hormonal teenage girl. It didn't matter what time it was. He'd start with his usual ramble: "I was one of those stupid fuckers once." "They grow out of it." "They mean well." "They're just boys."

I'd fire back, "Doesn't make it right."

He always had the same answer: "Give them grace."

Never.

"They repress everything."

Sounds like a them problem.

"Next time a boy's acting a fool, remember—there's always something soft underneath."

And I couldn't argue. Because my dad was proof. He used to be that guy—the frat bro who'd rather break his hand punching drywall than go to therapy. But he swore the day I was born, everything changed. I believed him. I've never seen that version of him. Now, he cries at award ceremonies and holiday concerts. He weeps over every milestone. I loved him for that.

Shaking off the memory, I would picture his stupid face as the ball and smacked it offset, but it had a satisfying clink against the aluminum. I watched it fly off to the side until it was no longer visible and made contact with a tree.

"You don't hesitate. You just commit. Slow down, and watch. You have to set it up nice and easy. Take a practice swing if you need to, but don't rush." Finishing his words of wisdom, he made perfect contact, and the ball soared into the night sky.

My father used to remark that my commitment and lack of hesitation were things he was proud of. But over the years, he turned it against me somewhere along the way. Like something I should be cautious about. Whatever, I don't see it as a weakness. I did the same process I had at first and hit it almost identical to his drive, "Looks like I don't need to."

With a scoff and a quick side hug. "Don't get cocky. Took practice to get there."

I rolled my eyes. When he went inside, I kept hitting balls, thinking about how easy boys—and men—are to manipulate. He was right. I don't hesitate to do things to get my way.

Dad taught me to observe, to notice the small things. Collecting boys became a game, like trading cards. I had to be careful, strategic. Each one had strengths I could use while bringing them to their knees. Once they served their purpose, I'd blame my family issues. I'd been lying to Edie about them for years—why not use that as my out? They never questioned it. They were boys. They knew how to move on.

I wasn't always like this. I could blame the Country Club. Watching older men ogle me like a bar cart girl was disgusting—but in some twisted way, I loved the attention, the power I had. They never turn into men, they're all boys wanting to be loved, to feel valued in a woman's life. These wrinkly old geezers would grab my waist too tight in greeting and whisper with their decaying teeth breath in my ear, "So mature for your age." "You've been growing haven't you." They would jeer hugging me tight to feel my growing breasts, and somehow, I kept smiling. Even thanked them. On the inside, I wanted to slit my wrists and have the blood spray all over them to teach them a lesson in what hitting on underage girls can do to a growing woman. Making me grow up quickly wasn't what I wanted, but I can't say it didn't increase my confidence. I learned to stand taller every time one of those assholes teed off into his own private hell.

Sometimes I wanted to scream at my family, how much they

suffocated me. But they were mine. Flawed, overwhelming, but mine. I thought distance would fix everything. Eighteen years of love felt like a chokehold. I thought a break would help us all. Typical teenage logic.

But looking back, I made mistakes.

I think about every cruel thing I said. Every time I made them feel small. Regret hits like a Rolodex of cuts. My parents weren't perfect, but they were present. They gave me everything they had.

With Edie, I'd say awful things about them just to match her suffering. Her broken home versus my, for the most part, normal family felt unfair. So I would drag my family's benign issues into the conversation. Since we were barely out of elementary school, we trauma-bonded over shitty parents. I'd always feel guilty and disgusted at myself for making mountains out of molehills, but it was nice to watch the weight on Edie's shoulders melt away.

Last night, after banging out my issues with Stephen, I left with my usual bittersweet feeling of being unsatisfied in pleasure but satisfied I regained control over his attention and affection. It's too late at this point, so I fully plan to see Mom, pissed off, waiting on the porch to scold me for missing curfew. I rolled down the driveway at a turtle's pace. Bracing myself for the worst. Her foot tapping in that way that always drove me insane, all revved up. But that was alright. Turning into her little girl with a slight baby voice would make her roll her eyes, but that meant I had her where I wanted her. Works every time.

I was in the middle of figuring out my script—how to soften the blow, what tone to use—when I saw flashing blue and white lights through the trees. Spinning. Violent. Too many.

I didn't turn off the ignition. Just threw the car in park and ran.

"I fucking live here!" I screamed, shoving past the first cop.

Another grabbed me before I reached the porch.

I didn't hear a word he said. All I could hear was my heart trying to beat its way out of my chest. The front yard was crawling with first responders—clipboards, radios, sidearms, all of it.

I pushed the cop. I didn't care.

"What happened?"

"You should stay out here," he said, jaw tight. "We need to confirm some things."

"Confirm this," I snapped, flipping him off and shoving past. I ran for the door.

The house was quiet—not the peaceful kind, but the kind that screams something's missing.

"Mom!" I called, voice cracking. "Dad!"

Heads turned. No one answered. From behind, a hand latched on my shoulder. I recoiled, knocking a picture frame off the wall. Glass shattered.

"Shit!"

"Sorry, Syl—it's just me." Butch. Our semi-homeless neighbor. Eyes red. Hands shaking.

"Where are they? What's going on?"

He hesitated. "I don't know how else to say this."

"Butch—tell me."

"I heard the alarm. It wouldn't stop. I came running and..." His voice broke. "I found him. Your dad—downstairs. I called 911. They found your mom upstairs. It's... it's bad, Sylvia. I'm so sorry."

His voice turned to high pitch static as I bolted toward the nearest cop, grabbing his vest and shaking him. "What happened to my parents?!"

He raised his hands, words scrambling behind his eyes. I was about to slap him when a detective tapped my bicep.

"I'm sorry for your loss, Ms. Harrington."

"What happened?" I pleaded.

He hesitated. "I don't know if now is the right—"

"What happened?" I shouted, my throat burning.

The detective's shoulders slumped. "It appears to be a home invasion. We're still investigating."

The words floated there. Cold. Clinical.

"No."

The world tunneled into black. My brain shut down. All I could see were memories—flashes, fragments. They couldn't be dead. You don't believe it until the bodies are rolled out in white sheets.

I stared at the detective, rage blooming hot in my chest.

"You better find the fucker who did this."

I wanted them back.

Chapter Twenty-Five

I was twenty, but my body felt sixty. My back ached, my limbs throbbed, and the dirt caked on my skin turned every movement into a struggle. I couldn't even risk taking a shit, no matter how much my stomach cramped—there wasn't space for it anyway. Everything was filthy. And those bitches didn't care.

I heard them outside the door, laughing about some hot professor. Fall break was over. That meant people were back. I screamed once, testing if anyone could hear me. They did. One of them beat me unconscious for it.

Syl gagged me after that. Her underwear stuffed in my mouth, sealed with duct tape. In another context, it might've been sexy. Instead, it tasted rancid, the stench burning its way into my sinuses. I woke up choking every time a bit of lace slipped loose and tickled the back of my throat.

Eventually, I stopped trying to scream.

Penelope woke me by shaking my shoulder hard enough to rattle the pain in my skull. "Wake up!" she hissed, ripping off the duct tape. "Why does your face look like it's falling off?"

"I can't hear you," I croaked. My ears still rang.

"Just fucking listen. Sylvia wants to kill you. Like, actually kill you. Soon."

Something inside me cracked. "Sorry to inconvenience y'all," I muttered. "Should I let myself out?"

Penelope glared, lowering her voice to a harsh whisper. "Harriet talked to me. She thinks this has gone too far. She wants to let you go."

I stared at her, disbelieving. "Why?"

"She's logical. Harry knows you don't deserve to die. That's enough for me. But Sylvia… she's changed. She's obsessed. And Emberly—" Penelope shuddered. "She's enjoying this too much to give up."

"Like you weren't?"

"Look, we all do what we have to do to survive. I wanted out. I couldn't. Sylvia paid me too much. And this school—this fucked-up school—it's not as simple as dropping out. It has a grip on all of us. I won't be sent to Isolation again for going against Discordia's acolytes."

"Acolytes? What the hell do they have to do with—"

"Doesn't matter now. They allow a lot here—but only with permission."

I let out a bitter laugh. "And you think since you don't have permission, that will be what convinces Sylvia to let me go? That's the dumbest thing I've ever heard. She thinks I killed her parents, Penelope. She's going to kill me. There's no way she's letting me out."

Penelope slapped me. My head snapped sideways. Pain bloomed like fireworks behind my eyes.

"Do you want my help or not?" she snapped.

"Harriet's trying. I'm trying. Or would you rather just bleed out and die?"

"Yes," I whispered. "Fine. Yes."

She wrinkled her nose. "You smell like shit." Then curled up in the corner by the door and said nothing else.

Sleep clawed at me, but the cold gnawed harder. The soil beneath me was nearly frozen. My teeth chattered, and I thought of those old nightmares where my teeth crumbled out of my mouth. I wondered if they'd actually fall out now—brittle from dehydration and frost.

Penelope wasn't the answer. Harriet wasn't either. And Emberly… Emberly was a nightmare made flesh.

She always took night watch. I don't know if she was an insomniac or just a sadist, but she made sure I never forgot she was there. If she wasn't poking or taunting me, she was staring—unblinking—as if willing my soul to splinter.

Maybe it was working.

After her last round, I drifted into a haze. I wanted to be anywhere else. Somewhere warm. Somewhere safe.

Instead, I was cold, filthy, and bleeding.

When Penelope came back, she was quiet. Paler. Her eyes darted like prey.

"Tomorrow morning," she whispered.

"What?"

"Sylvia said at dinner it would be tomorrow. You're not leaving here, Edith. She's going to—"

"Oh." The word fell flat.

"I'm sorry," she said. It sounded real, or maybe I wanted it to.

Her hand rested on my shoulder, her eyes glistening

with what might have been guilt—or maybe nothing at all.

The door creaked open.

I cringed as Sylvia and Emberly walked in. Penelope yanked her hand away, standing stiffly like a child caught breaking curfew.

Sylvia didn't even look at me. She focused on Penelope instead, her smile icy. "I'm impressed," she said, stepping closer.

I barely registered what Emberly was holding until she raised it over her head. A baseball bat length of wood with nails jutting out.

I squeezed my eyes shut.

The first crack echoed. Penelope crumpled.

Sylvia murmured her approval as Emberly swung again. And again. Blood sprayed as she tore the makeshift weapon free, over and over.

I couldn't look away.

The pool beneath Penelope's skull shimmered red against the frozen dirt. The sound was sharp, wet, and endless.

Thwack. Thwack. Thwack. Until there was no face left.

When it stopped, the silence screamed louder than the violence.

Sylvia loomed over her, one boot crushing Penelope's ruined face. I heard the wet squelch of bone.

"Traitor," she said, sing-song sweet.

Then her eyes found mine—black and hollow.

"Oh, Edith," she cooed. "You thought you'd leave here alive?"

I didn't answer. I couldn't.

Sylvia crouched in front of me, her face inches from mine. "You're going to die," she whispered. "Tomorrow morning. But don't worry. That?" She gestured to Penelope's body. "That was the easy part."

She smiled—gleeful, hateful, cruel. Then they left me there. Alone. With what was left of Penelope.

I cried until I couldn't stop weeping for hours until the tears ran out and my body was spent.

***

They left me alone the rest of the day and night. My body would not stop screaming at me. My ribs throbbed, my broken arm hung limp, and the soil under me was soaked with blood, piss, and sweat.

Penelope's last words still echoed in my head. "Tomorrow morning." Sylvia would kill me tomorrow.

I don't know how long I stared at the ceiling before I heard them. Three sets of footsteps.

The door creaked. Cold air swept in. My body trembled. I couldn't move. My head lolled. I saw them— Sylvia in front, Emberly behind her with the bloodstained two-by-four, and Harriet trailing.

Sylvia stood in front, her posture impossibly straight. Her hair gleamed under the dim bulb, her sharp black eyes focused on me. Emberly had the two-by-four she'd used to kill Penelope slung over one shoulder, her grin cocky and cruel. Harriet's face was drained of color. She backed away, trying to wrestle her expression into something neutral.

Sylvia stood in front of me, so close I could see the faint smudge of mascara under her left eye. "You're quiet," she said softly. "Finally."

I didn't respond. I didn't have the strength to.

Her smile widened, but it didn't reach her eyes. "You know, Edith, I used to think you were clever. Manipulative, yes, but clever. Now I see you for what you are—pathetic. Weak. And a killer."

"That's not true," I croaked.

She leaned in. "You killed my parents."

The words hit like a slap. But she didn't want the truth. She wanted a confession.

"Why don't you just do it already?" I rasped.

Her smile vanished. "Cut her down."

Emberly dropped the rope from the pipe. My body collapsed. Sylvia straddled me, her knees pinning me down. I thrashed, useless.

She pulled something from her pocket.

A blade.

"Don't," I whispered.

She ignored me. Gripped my jaw, forced me to look at her.

"You don't get to beg," she said. "You didn't give *them* mercy."

The first stab was clean—into my side. Fire lit my veins. I gasped.

Then again.

And again.

I lost count.

Pain blurred everything. My heartbeat slowed, ears ringing.

I thought of sunlight. The way it felt when I first got here. I wondered if I'd ever feel that again.

Sylvia leaned close, her breath warm against my ear.

"Why wait 'til morning, this is justice," she whispered.

The world was slipping away. My vision narrowed, the edges darkening like an old photograph. My last thought was simple, unspoken.

I didn't kill them.

***

Sylvia stood, her chest rising and falling with the effort it took to breathe. Blood was everywhere—on her hands, her shirt, even the knife. Edith lay still, her eyes half-open but vacant.

She wiped the blade on her jeans. Her hands shook. "Harriet," she said. "Help me move her."

Harriet didn't budge. She stared at Edith's body, lips parted.

"Harriet," Sylvia snapped.

She flinched. Nodded. Emberly dragged Penelope's body toward the far corner of the basement, muttering something under her breath about how heavy she was.

Sylvia didn't watch. She didn't want to.

"We burn the clothes," she said, her voice mechanical. "We get the acid. We stick to the plan."

Her hands were still shaking, so she clasped them behind her back. She couldn't afford to fall apart now.

Harriet stopped mid-step, her voice cracking. "What do we do if someone… finds out?"

"They won't." Sylvia's voice was colder than she felt.

Emberly laughed from across the room, tossing the two-by-four into the corner. "Even if they do, we'll handle it. We're smarter than that."

Sylvia didn't respond. She stared at Edith's body

instead, her stomach churning.

***

The three of them stood in a loose circle around Edith and Penelope's bodies. Emberly was grinning, Harriet was pale, and Sylvia... Sylvia couldn't let herself feel anything.

"We stick to the plan," Sylvia said finally. "No one talks. No one slips."

"What about Penelope?" Harriet whispered.

"What about her?" Emberly snapped.

"She was one of us."

"She made her choice," Sylvia said. Final.

Harriet didn't argue. She stared at the ground, her shoulders slumping.

Sylvia took a deep breath, her mind racing through the steps ahead. Burn the clothes. Get the acid. Dig deep enough somewhere that no one would ever find the bodies. First step, clean house.

And then? Well, she didn't know that. She could barely comprehend beyond tomorrow. Disposal would have to come later.

"Let's get to work, first thing tomorrow" she said.

***

Disposal would have to come later.

Sylvia sat at the kitchen table, staring at an untouched mug of tea. The others were asleep—or pretending. She didn't care.

She rubbed her temples. Her hands still felt sticky with phantom blood.

173

No one's coming for you. No one knows.
It didn't feel like reassurance anymore.
It felt like a lie.

Chapter Twenty-Six

Before

I had to know where she was going. What if she was being reckless?

There was a moment—just a moment—when I could've sworn Syl looked right at me. She was straddling some loser in his busted-up Mustang, putting on her little show. I couldn't stand it—watching her pretend. I had to keep reminding myself it wasn't real. She's into me.

She'll see soon. She'll know it's always been me. I love her too much for her not to love me back. In time, she will.

I left before I screamed or did something that'd blow my cover. She'll come to her senses. She has to. I've been here, waiting. Doesn't she see everything I've done for her?

My phone buzzed in my hand, lighting up with our last exchange.

Hey, can we hang out? I know it's late, but mom is being a bitch.

Her reply came instantly:

Sure.

That one word made my stomach twist. Sure. Syl never texted like that. One-word answers weren't her thing. She was distracted, that's all. At least she said yes.

I always kept an overnight bag in my car, just in case she ever caved and let me sleep beside her again. Too bad her parents were still clinging to their delusions. I'd be lying if I said I wasn't in love with Syl—romantically, physically. Maybe her parents saw it before I did. Doesn't mean they weren't awful.

As I drove to her house, I ran my fingers over the strap of the bag, tracing the frayed edges.

I couldn't wait to see her.

By the time I got to her door, rain had soaked me through. She gave me a quick side-hug—the kind that left a dull ache in my chest—and let me in without a word.

I headed straight to her bathroom to shower, peeling off my wet clothes, letting the scalding water wash off the guilt. I imagined her joining me, her body sliding beneath the spray, close enough to breathe in.

The door creaked.

My heart jumped. The curtain was fogged but see-through. I turned, expecting her.

There she was, stepping closer.

For one glorious second, I thought—this is it.

Then she yanked the curtain aside, her eyes locked on mine.

"Why were you following me?"

The words hit like a slap.

"What?"

"You know what I'm talking about," she said, voice low, sharp.

"Syl, I—"

"Don't. Don't lie to me, Edith."

She folded her arms, glaring. I could barely breathe.

"Edie, we've been best friends forever, but I can't do this anymore. I can't keep pretending I don't see what's going on. You're obsessed with me. It's not normal. It's not okay."

I opened my mouth to speak, but she cut me off.

"Let me finish. You've been acting weird since graduation, since you told me how you felt. I tried to let you down easy, but you won't let it go. And now… now I find out you've been following me?"

"I wasn't——"

"Shut up, Edie. Just shut up."

Her voice cracked, but her eyes didn't waver.

"I'm straight. I've told you this before. Even if I weren't, I still wouldn't be into you. I love you, but not the way you want me to. And you can't keep doing this. To me. To us."

I wanted to say something. Anything. But my throat was sandpaper.

"You need to leave," she said. "After your shower, just… go."

"Syl…"

"No. I mean it. We're done."

She turned and walked out, leaving the door open.

The cold air hit my skin like punishment. I stood there, dripping, mind racing.

She doesn't love me. She never did.

But I could fix this. I could fix us.

The plan formed before I even stepped out of the shower.

Sylvia's parents. They were always the problem. If they were gone, she'd finally see the truth.

She'd see me.

***

In my fantasies, we built a life together. I'd lead her away from her awful parents, her toxic habits. I'd be her salvation.

I wanted to live inside her—her mind, her body, carried around in her thoughts. I wanted to wake up with her, feel her soft, sleepy warmth as she dragged me to breakfast. I wanted to spend hours with her at the bookstore, sipping espresso and watching her get adorably irritated about nothing.

Sylvia doesn't see the vision, but that's okay. I've always been more patient than her.

I have kept playing my role perfectly. The doting best friend. The quiet observer. Shutting up when it came to her mentioning guys she's talking to. I'd done it for her sake and she seemed to accept what I put out, but it wasn't real with me either and I played ignorant to anything different.

It was the night of graduation when everything cracked. We were at the diner, eating pancakes at midnight. I couldn't hold it in anymore. I told her how I felt. Stupid. I stopped pretending—and she shattered me.

But men get to be persistent, don't they? They show up with flowers, boom boxes, and declarations. Why can't I? I just need to show her she's worth fighting for.

I parked nearby and slipped through the woods toward her house. The bamboo patch was black as pitch—perfect cover. From here, I had a clear view of her parents' bedroom. They'd left the blinds open again.

I hated them. Mr. Harrington with his bloated gut and gambling debt. Mrs. Harrington wasting money and dragging Syl to church like that would fix her. They were the kind of people who bake chicken without seasoning. Dry. Bland. Pointless.

They didn't deserve her. Watching them was like watching a terrible TV show—characters doing nothing they should and nothing ever gets better. It just sucks, but you still stick around for the next episode because what if they finally change? I wonder if Syl feels the same.

My binoculars caught movement in the window. Them again, going at it like rabbits. Mr. Harrington thrust like a man trying to prove something, and Mrs. Harrington faked her moans. Like mother like daughter I guess.

I wanted to puke.

Her car pulled into the driveway like clockwork, headlights slicing through the rain. I wonder if she knows I'm here. She'd already caught me once now and I barely got her to forgive me after spamming her with texts and calls for five consecutive days. Just like other times. Does she expect this of me now? She said we were done, but I still don't believe her performance. She's a shitty actress.

CHAPTER TWENTY-SEVEN

Sylvia

I couldn't sleep. Three showers, each hotter than the last, and I still felt blood on my hands. My chest was tight, my head pounding, and no amount of pacing or breathwork could silence the thought looping through my brain.

What if someone finds them?

We'd rehearsed the plan a hundred times—burn the clothes, buy supplies from different stores, dig deep. But that was before Penelope. Now there were two bodies and one less pair of hands to bury them.

Emberly's snores were deafening, each one grating like sandpaper and knotting tension in my joints. I stared at the popcorn ceiling, tracing imaginary escape routes that led nowhere.

No one is coming for you. No one knows.

I told myself that again and again, but the knot in my stomach wouldn't loosen. Edith was dead. Penelope was dead. And it was my job to keep them that way—buried, literally and otherwise.

I exhaled slowly. Counted to five. Inhaled again. Useless.

My parents' faces flashed in my mind. Would they be proud of me if they knew what I'd done? My throat tightened.

Of course not.

But maybe… maybe they'd understand.

The tears came without warning—hot and stinging as they slid into my ears. I wiped them away angrily. I didn't have time for this.

Shoving the blanket aside, I slid to the edge of the bed. A cramp shot through my calf as I stood, and I bit my lip to keep from crying out. When it passed, I moved quickly, grabbing my coat and slippers without waking Emberly.

The door creaked as I opened it. I froze, heart pounding, but no one stirred. Carefully, I slipped out into the hallway.

The kitchen was cold, the kind of chill that crept into your bones and stayed there. I filled the kettle and set it on the stove, then rummaged through the cabinet for tea.

Penelope's teacup caught my eye—the one with gaudy pink swirls and gold accents. I remembered the time she'd yanked my hair for touching it. *"A poor person's touch ruins the glaze,"* she'd said.

I snorted at the memory. But the smile curdled fast. She was a bitch—but she was our bitch. *My* bitch.

And I killed her.

Not directly, maybe. But I didn't stop it either.

Pen betrayed us, I reminded myself. *She betrayed me.*

The kettle whistled. I poured the water over a peach-mint bag, letting the steam kiss my face. Set a five-minute timer. Turned to the window and stood on tiptoe to scan the parking lot.

Even this late, people were coming and going. No one looked suspicious. No sirens. No nosy neighbors.

We kept Edith locked in the basement for three weeks, and no one noticed. That should've comforted me.

Instead, my chest tightened further.

The timer beeped, jolting me. I fished out the tea bag, laid it on a plate. My mom used to say you could reuse a tea bag four times. *A poverty trick,* she'd called it. But I liked the second steep best—clean, simple, not bitter.

Too bad no amount of tea could wash away what I'd done.

I carried the cup to the table, wrapping my hands around it. The warmth bled into my palms. The pounding in my ears had finally stopped—but the silence was worse. It pressed in, thick and cloying.

Killing Edith was supposed to solve everything. Retribution. Justice. Closure. Call it what you want.

But all I felt was cold.

Edith wasn't innocent. She'd latched onto me for years like a parasite, sucking the air out of every room we entered. And she *did* kill my parents. I didn't care if there wasn't proof. I knew.

But knowing didn't make it easier.

I thought about the night before prom, how she scared off my date with her obsessive act. I remembered the time I caught her dissecting a snake and feeding the pieces to her dog. And then there was that day after our sleepover. She looked like a maniac.

My stomach turned. I hadn't let myself remember that day for years, but now it was clawing its way to the surface.

Edith with blood all over her face. Practically salivating with my menstrual blood dripping into her mouth. That's all I could remember before everything went black. I've tried for years to remember what happened, but there's only one answer. *She* did it. Thinking violence would clean up her mess. But I remember.

That was the first time I truly understood what she was capable of. I tried to ice her out, but she persisted.

And still, for some god forsaken reason, I let her back into my life.

***

The tea had gone cold, but I didn't care. My thoughts spiraled, twisting in on themselves, looping with no beginning or end.

I had to move. Had to breathe.

I grabbed my coat again and stepped into the yard. The screen door slammed behind me. I flinched. Prayed no one heard.

The night air sliced through me, but I welcomed it. I walked to the edge of the cemetery. My slippers crunched against the gravel, aimless steps in the dark. That was fine. I didn't want to stop.

Penelope's body. Edith's body. The smell. The rot. The basement.

It was all waiting for me.

Halloween was in two days. The RAs would be doing inspections. That was the deal—no alcohol, no boys, and definitely no corpses in the building.

We'd gotten lucky so far. But luck never lasted.

I stopped walking. My breath puffed clouds into the air. I didn't have room for more mistakes.

If I wanted to survive—really survive—I had to act.

Emberly and Harriet could help. For now. But once the bodies were gone, I wouldn't need them anymore.

I scratched at something sticky on my sleeve. Was that blood? Jam? I couldn't remember the last time I ate.

I turned back toward the house, jaw clenched.

I'd figure this out.

I had to.

Chapter Twenty-Eight

Sylvia

The crackling of dead leaves sent shocks into my joints, a tension that settled in my shoulders and refused to leave. The sound was everywhere—scraping, echoing—and I couldn't tell if it had always been there or if I was finally losing my mind.

We still didn't have a plan that would leave us unscathed. It was driving me fucking insane. I sat rigid on the couch, staring into the kitchen. My skin crawled like it was infested, and no matter how I tried to redirect my thoughts, they circled back to the bodies rotting beneath the floorboards.

The silence was unbearable. My ears rang with a high, piercing tone, like a wire stretched too tight. I'd tried to sleep, tried to breathe, tried every grounding trick I knew—but every time I closed my eyes, I saw their decaying faces. Every attempt to put myself at ease had failed.

I'd been sitting there, paralyzed, when I heard

Harriet's footsteps pattering down the servant stairwell. I bolted upright, suddenly desperate to speak to someone—anyone—to get out of my head.

Harriet walked in, her sage green silk pajamas flowing with every step. She didn't even glance my way. "How'd you sleep?" she asked, her tone maddeningly calm.

"Horribly. You?"

"Soundly."

"Oh."

"Oh?" she echoed, flatly.

I snapped. "Harry, are you seriously not worried? Penelope and Edith are *down there*, decomposing, and we still have no idea what the fuck to do with them! The smell is so rancid I couldn't be in the basement for more than a second. I almost puked!"

Harriet didn't flinch. She pulled out the kettle, filled it, and placed it on the stove—every movement practiced and glacial. "One scoop of sugar or two?"

"Harriet!"

She turned finally, raising a single eyebrow. "Sylvia, you need to calm down. It's morning. We have time."

"Time for *what*? I'm barely holding it together. We were strained with one body and four of us, now it's two bodies and three of us!"

Her expression didn't change. "It's alright. I have an idea if you'd like to hear it."

"No, Harry, I wouldn't."

She ignored the sarcasm. "Yes, Harry, please share your brilliant idea. Because I have *nothing*."

"Let's talk it over breakfast," she said, sliding a prepared casserole dish from the fridge like it had been waiting there all night.

"When the hell did you make that?"

"Before bed. It takes about an hour to bake, so don't wake Emberly."

"I'm not asleep," Emberly called from the hallway, startling me. She strolled into the kitchen, grinning, then kissed me—quickly but deeply.

"Jesus Christ, Em!"

"Not my fault you're oblivious—ooh, what's that?"

"French toast casserole," Harriet replied.

"Nice. I'll be quick in the shower. Don't plan my murder while I'm gone." She winked and swung herself around the banister, nearly taking the rug with her.

"Too soon?" she called.

"Too soon," I muttered.

Harriet didn't react as I turned back to her, muttering under my breath. The kettle whistled, and she calmly poured water over the tea bags as if we weren't all about to lose our minds.

***

The oven dinged, and Harriet retrieved the casserole as Emberly came back downstairs. The smell of cinnamon and vanilla filled the air, making my stomach twist painfully. I realized I hadn't eaten.

We sat down together, the warmth of the food giving us a moment of false peace. For a second, it almost felt normal.

But none of this was normal.

After a few forced bites, I broke the silence. "We all know inspections are coming. I thought I could figure this out, but it's falling apart. I don't know what to do."

Silence.

Harriet set her fork down.

"We could dissolve them with acid," she said. "We'd need to dismember them and use sealed containers. The decomposition should help. A cleaver will be fine."

Emberly and I exchanged glances. Harriet just sipped her tea, perfectly composed.

"That… doesn't sound terrible," I admitted, hesitant.

Emberly frowned. "Yeah, but what about the containers? The leftover acid? What if something's left— like teeth?"

Harriet met her gaze without blinking. "Teeth can be pulverized. We'll scatter the remains in different places. Unless you have a better idea, Emberly?"

"I'm just saying, if this goes sideways, we're all fucked. So we adapt. We all help prep. Make it quick work. Later we separate to get supplies."

I leaned forward, gripping my mug. "So you'll stay behind? To get them… ready?"

"Fine with me."

I exhaled shakily. "And you *really* think this will work, Harry?"

Harriet looked at me sharply. "Nothing ever works perfectly, Sylvia. But it's the best option."

It wasn't comforting, but it was enough. For now.

***

Just as we were finishing breakfast, the doorbell rang.

My heart stopped.

The three of us locked eyes, the air in the room thick

with unspoken fear. I stood slowly, willing my legs not to tremble as I walked to the door.

It was the RA, clipboard in hand, chewing gum loudly.

"Hey, Syl! Just here to let you know you'll be getting a new flatmate soon. Should arrive between today and tomorrow. You alright? You look a little pale..."

I forced a smile, praying she didn't hear the pounding of my heart. "I'm fine. Thanks for letting me know."

She left with a cheerful wave, and I shut the door and leaned against it, exhaling in a long, trembling breath.

Emberly appeared beside me, her face creased with concern. "Everything okay?"

"No," I whispered.

Then it hit me all at once.

I grabbed a pillow and started swinging. Screaming. The room became a blur—glass shattered, books flew, furniture slammed into walls.

I reached for the coffee table, ready to send it through the bay window—when Emberly tackled me to the floor.

The impact knocked the breath from my lungs. For a second, everything was still.

"We'll fix this," she murmured into my ear.

I didn't know if I believed her.

CHAPTER TWENTY-NINE

Sylvia

Harriet paced for the first time in her life, her usual composure cracked by my meltdown. Emberly sat beside me on the floor, her hands on my shoulders, steady but fading. Her patience thinned by the second.

I chewed my nails to the quick, my voice breaking. "What do we do? I wasn't ready for this. We didn't plan for this."

Emberly tried to soothe me. "How could we have? No one expects to be hiding *bodies* in the basement. We'll figure it out."

My breathing hitched. "Oh God, this already sounds like it's in the news. The journalists are probably already on their way, asking for fucking interviews!"

I smacked my forehead with the heel of my palm. Emberly grabbed my wrist gently.

"Alright, stop. First—we clean. Harriet, take your room. I'll do the bathrooms and sweep. Sylvia, just… focus on the living room."

I wiped my face with trembling hands. The pressure pressed down on me like wet cement—Edith's corpse, Penelope's body, and now the imminent arrival of a stranger. I couldn't even summon gratitude that Harriet and Emberly were still helping. The guilt gnawed at me instead.

Harriet didn't need prompting. She went to the closet and pulled out supplies: brooms, spray bottles, gloves, paper towels. Then she added a Bluetooth speaker, and soon the sharp swell of Tchaikovsky filled the flat.

"Classical?" Emberly raised a brow, leaning on the kitchen counter. "Didn't peg you as the 'clean to violins' type."

"I'm a proactive planner, not a firefighter," Harriet replied.

"And that means…?"

"It means," Harriet said, snapping on gloves, "classical music reduces violent tendencies. A lot of low-income shops use it to keep unhoused people from loitering. Consider it a strategy—preventing another Sylvia tantrum."

"Good luck with that," Emberly muttered.

Still crouched among the shattered glass, I snapped, "I can *hear* you, you know."

Harriet hummed indifferently as she headed upstairs, her footsteps as sharp as her tone.

My focus scattered, my movements mechanical. I swept glass into a dustpan at a glacial pace. Emberly returned and crouched beside me.

"Need help?"

"No."

"Babe, come on." She touched my arm, and I flinched.

"I said I'm *fine*," I hissed, eyes averted. "Go clean the fucking bathroom. Leave me alone."

Emberly froze, her jaw tightening. Grabbing my wrist, her voice sunk low. Cutting deep.

"I killed for you. Do you get that? *Killed*. That's loyalty. And this is how you treat me? You don't bleed on the people who didn't cut you, Syl."

She let go, straightened. "If you don't want help, fine. But you better act like you're not trying to take the rest of us down with you."

I stared, stunned, as she turned and stomped up the stairs. People say they would kill for each other as a metaphor. But I knew she really meant it.

Silence followed—except for the violins and my soft sobs. I let them fall for a few minutes, face buried in my hands. Wiping my face, I stood, and forced myself back to work.

***

By mid-afternoon, the flat smelled like lemon cleaner and sweat. The silence was tense. No one spoke unless it was necessary. I scoured the walls for dents and scratches to repair, while Emberly mopped and Harriet sorted through boxes in the spare room.

I leaned against the kitchen counter, sipping water and willing my throat to swallow as I stared out the window. The world outside seemed impossibly distant. Women walked past our building, laughing, carrying shopping bags, living lives untouched by this nightmare.

Any one of them could be the new roommate.

The thought made my stomach twist.

I needed air. I grabbed a cigarette, stepped onto the porch, and lit up. My hands trembled as I inhaled.

What now? We didn't have time to pull this off before the new girl showed up. Burying the bodies nearby was too risky—too many eyes, too many unknowns. But what was the alternative?

My thoughts spiraled. I took one last drag, crushed the cigarette, and bolted upstairs, boots thudding against the steps.

I found Harriet in her room, reorganizing her bookshelf.

"I have a plan," I blurted.

She turned, one brow arched.

"It's simple. Tomorrow night, I'll go to Passenger's Peak—after dark. I'll bury the bodies there. No one hikes that late. You and Emberly just prep the basement. Wrap the bodies in tarps or whatever. I'll dig the holes at dusk— it's fucking Halloween and it's not broad daylight. Then I'll come back, grab the bodies, and drop them. All *you* have to do is restore the basement once I take them. Fast. Clean. And we're done. For good."

Harriet frowned. "Why you? Alone? That's dangerous. What if the RA checks before you're back?"

"I'll be fast. And if I *am* caught digging, what are they going to do? Slap me on the wrist for disturbing the dirt? If anything goes wrong, it's on me. You've already done enough, just play dumb."

"You even know the terrain? The park's been redone."

I waved her off. "I'll scout it during the day. Halloween's perfect—everyone will be distracted. By the time I load the bodies, everyone will be partying."

Harriet was silent for a long moment. Finally, she said, "It's risky. But it could work."

I knew that if Harriet thought it could, we had a solid chance.

***

That evening, the three of them gathered in the living room. I outlined the plan again, this time more composed. Emberly listened, leaning back in her chair with a smirk.

"Wow," she said after I finished, "That's actually sweet. My heart."

"Fuck you."

"There she is." Emberly laughed and stood, stretching. "Alright, boss. I'm in."

Harriet nodded. "I'll help. But think this through, Sylvia. Impulse gets people caught."

"I'm *not* being impulsive," I snapped.

Harriet didn't blink. "Then prove it."

My chest heaved, but she turned and climbed the stairs without another word.

***

The shower scalded my skin, and I welcomed the burn. It made me feel clean. Real. I leaned against the wall, letting the water hit my face until I couldn't breathe.

For a moment, I felt empty—no guilt, no fear, just silence. Sure, Edith was an enormous part of my life. Yes, at one time, I cared deeply for her. Like a *sister*. It might be seen as an opinion, but I knew the truth. Edith was demented and a murderer. Those sick and twisted games to sink her claws in me was over. She can't hurt me anymore. None of the good moments could outweigh all the horrible things she had done, no telling what Edith was up to when we weren't together.

The weight of my actions crept back in as soon as she stepped out. Wrapping myself in a towel, I stared at my reflection in the foggy mirror.

"You'll make this right," I whispered, "you have to."

My reflection stayed silent.

Chapter Thirty

Sylvia

I yanked at the duct tape, the harsh rip echoing through the silence. It wasn't enough to hold Penelope together, but it would have to do. Emberly dragged the bodies into position, her boots crunching over the dirt floor. The smell was unbearable—a stomach-turning blend of soil, rot, and something sweet beneath it. The bugs had already begun their work, their tiny movements visible in the dim light.

Hours later, the basement reeked of bleach and death. The stench clung to my skin, my hair, my lungs.

Penelope and Edith were wrapped in plastic, sealed in duct tape. One step closer.

Harriet hovered nearby, yellow rubber gloves pulled high on her forearms. Her face was flushed of all color, her breathing shallow and fast.

I shoved the door open, grabbing the pink and red blankets I snagged from Penelope's room. She won't miss them. "This is all I could find," I muttered before darting back outside to retrieve the tarp.

Emberly's voice was steady, cold. "Let's get it done."

Harriet flinched but nodded. "Right. Yeah. Okay." Though the room was stifling, she rubbed her arms like she couldn't get warm.

Together, Emberly and Harriet maneuvered the first body onto the blanket. I dropped to my knees beside them, folding the corners tight, burrito-style. My movements were sharp, clinical. The duct tape screeched as I wound it around the ankles, torso, and head. Harriet winced with every pull.

"I don't think I can—" she started.

"You can," I said flatly, not looking up.

By the time we turned to Edith's body, Harriet was swaying. She clamped a hand over her mouth. The sharp stench clawed its way into her lungs and wouldn't let go.

"I—I'll check outside," Harriet choked, backing toward the door.

I rolled my eyes, sweat stinging as it slid into them. "Harriet, we need all hands here."

"I can't," she whispered, her voice cracking. Then she bolted, the door slamming behind her like a punctuation mark.

My jaw clenched. "Unbelievable," I muttered, tying off the cling wrap around Edith's midsection. I wiped my hands clean on my dirt-smeared jeans, making them worse for wear. "We're on a clock. Let's move."

Emberly shrugged, grabbing another roll of tape. "She's not built for this."

"Who is?" I snapped, shoving the body into place with more force than necessary.

By the time we finished, my arms ached, and my breathing was shallow. We dragged the prepped bodies near the door, ready to load when the coast was clear. The room was nearly returned to its usual filth, save for the residual smell of sweat and rot. We dusted off our pants and couldn't help but double-check the space for any incriminating evidence.

With the bodies wrapped and ready, I grabbed my tote bag and fished out my car keys. I hadn't driven my own car in months. Emberly's had been my default ride while I "recovered" from everything. I pushed the thought down.

"Harriet's useless," I muttered. "I'm gonna go scout the site."

"Just be quick," Emberly said. "We can't afford any more surprises."

I snorted. "No pressure or anything."

Outside, Harriet leaned against the wall, trembling as she tore off her gloves. She pressed a palm to her stomach, trying to breathe. Her ears were probably still ringing from the sound of duct tape tearing again and again.

She stared at the treeline. Leaves rustled faintly. It didn't help.

When I joined her I saw her bite her lip hard enough to draw blood.

They need me. I have to help, even *if I hate it*, even *if it's wrong.*

***

My car sat untouched in the surplus lot, coated in dust and dead leaves. I slid into the driver's seat, my heart pounding as I turned the key. The engine sputtered, reluctant.

"Don't you dare," I hissed.

I tried again.

This time, it caught—shuddering to life like it was laughing at me. I gripped the wheel, exhaling hard.

The drive to Passenger's Peak was uneventful, but my thoughts weren't. They looped endlessly—Edith's face, the smell of decomp, the weight of guilt pressing on my chest.

I pressed the gas harder, weaving through traffic with frantic determination. My car felt like it was held together with chewing gum, each vibration a reminder of my precarious situation.

***

The park entrance loomed ahead, the narrow road flanked by towering trees. Cars lined up at the gate, waiting for it to open. I drummed my fingers on the steering wheel, my thoughts racing.

If we couldn't bury the bodies here, the entire plan would fall apart.

I swallowed the lump in my throat. Could we hide them on the slope? Dump them near the overlook? No. Too risky. Too exposed. Animals would get to them. Someone would find something.

They have to be buried. Deep. Gone.

The gate opened, and the line crawled forward. I inched past the ranger station, met the guy's eyes, forced a smile. He didn't smile back.

I parked in the first spot far from the crowd and checked my phone. Nothing from Emberly.

I called. My foot tapped with every ring.

"Hey," she answered.

"Why didn't you text back?"

"I've been running around for you," she snapped. "What now?"

"I need bolt cutters. Gloves. Spray paint. Shovel. Check your texts."

"Got it." Emberly hung up without another word.

I scowled at my phone. "Bitch," I muttered under my breath.

***

The trails were packed with hikers, families, and groups of friends snapping photos of the scenic overlooks. I kept my head down, blending into the crowd as best I could. I followed the natural rock stairs down to a fork in the trail. One path was steep and strenuous; the other looped around the peak.

I took the loop trail, walking with the slower crowd. Each step dragged. My lungs, unable to take a full breath. My heartbeat thudded in my ears.

Halfway through, I stopped.

The ground was rock. Compacted earth. Unmovable. No place to dig. No way to hide a thing.

"Fuck," I hissed. My hands curled into fists.

I finished the loop in a blur of rage. By the time I got to my car, I flung myself inside and slammed the door.

The engine roared to life on the first try. I rested my forehead against the wheel, my whole body shaking.

"God," I whispered. "I don't ask for much. Just let me survive this. Let this work. Let me have something."

***

Driving out of the park, I spotted an overgrown path branching off the main road. Curious, I turned down the dirt trail, my tires crunching over loose gravel. The trees thickened around me, their canopy blocking out the sun.

After a few minutes, the trail opened into a clearing. Rusted construction equipment sat abandoned in the tall grass. The ground was soft soil, untouched and secluded.

I stepped out of the car and scanned the area. There were no signs of people, hikers, or park rangers.

It was perfect.

I let out a shaky laugh and wiped my face with my sleeve. "Thank you," I whispered.

It wasn't flawless. But it was hope. And that was more than I'd had in days.

I turned the car around, memorizing every curve of the trail.

Now I just had to get back in time to pull it off.

Chapter Thirty-One

Sylvia

The afternoon passed in slow motion, but the new roommate still hadn't arrived. None of us dared to move. We didn't want to risk being caught off guard. I sat in the bay window, watching the sun sink lower and lower, golden light bleeding into dusk.

For hours, no one spoke. The silence wasn't peaceful—it was suffocating, thick enough to drown in. We'd done everything we could. All that was left was to believe the plan would hold.

It had to.

Two more trips, and this nightmare would be over. The first would take the longest—digging the graves. That was the riskiest part. The part where someone might see me. The second trip was just transport. A straight shot. By then, most students would be drunk or off campus, wrapped up in Halloween like it was some harmless night instead of one that could end your life.

I laced up my boots, the motion grounding me while

my mind spun.

"Harriet, you good?" I asked, eyes still fixed on the horizon.

She didn't answer right away. I waited, watching the light fade.

"As good as I can be," she said finally, voice far away.

I leaned forward, elbows resting on my knees. "I promise, Harry. It ends tonight. Once I come back for them, it's over. From there, you two are out. If I get caught, it's on me."

Harriet made one of those noncommittal humming sounds that always set my teeth on edge.

"What?" I asked, sharper than I meant.

"I just think… the evidence says otherwise. But hey—maybe I'm wrong."

"You're never wrong," Emberly said, voice tight.

Harriet shrugged. "There's a first time for everything."

I stood, exhaling slowly. "Doesn't matter. If I confess, they'll believe me. They won't come for you two. Just stay quiet. That's all I ask." I looked between them until they nodded.

"This is over tonight. One way or another. Do you trust me?"

They didn't answer, but I didn't need them to. Their silence was enough.

***

Emberly followed me to the car, her steps too soft to match the tension radiating off her. "You're sure about this?"

"I have to be." I shrugged, then added quietly, "I am. I love you."

"I love you too."

I kissed her. Not like usual. This one tasted like goodbye. I didn't meet her eyes after. Couldn't risk unraveling.

She loaded the supplies into the trunk while I climbed into the driver's seat. When she came to the window, she tapped the roof and leaned in. "That's everything. Spray paint included. Why'd you need it again?"

I wiped at my face, managing a weak laugh. "Oh, I don't anymore. Just—better safe than sorry."

She didn't look convinced, but she smiled. "Classic Sylvia."

"Classic," I echoed.

I backed out slowly, pausing beside her one last time. "I was gonna tag the gate if I had to break in. Cover my tracks."

She shook her head. "Sounds like you."

I laughed. And for a second, it felt almost real. "I'll be back soon."

She waved, worry plain in her eyes. She didn't know about the passport and plane ticket hidden in my waistband. When I was out of sight, I pulled them out and tossed them into the glove box.

***

The drive to the park felt endless. I passed the campers on the way up, their tents clustered near the mountain's base. My chest tightened when I saw them, but I forced myself to breathe. They wouldn't see me. They wouldn't even know I was here.

By the time I reached the clearing, the overgrown path looked just as it had earlier—hidden, untouched. Perfect.

I turned onto the dirt road, careful not to kick up dust. My headlights cut through the dark, sweeping across rusted equipment and tangled weeds. I parked and scanned the shadows. No cops. No hikers. Just me.

I grabbed the shovel and gear, stepping into the clearing. The old tractors and dump trucks loomed like rusted skeletons in the moonlight, silent witnesses to whatever I was about to do.

Back in the car, I stared at the glove box.

Why not just take the ticket and get the *fuck* out of here?

Let them decide who the killer was. Wouldn't matter since I would already have fled the country. It was enticing...

"Just dig," I muttered to myself, my voice swallowed by the dark.

Chapter Thirty-Two

Harriet sat frozen, rooted to the couch in a silence that felt ear-splitting. Emberly paced the living room, her boots thudding rhythmically on the worn wooden floor. The kettle hissed faintly in the kitchen—too soft to do anything about the tension choking the air.

Harriet thought about getting up. Checking the window. Moving to another room—but the thought never turned into action. Her body felt like a weight, sunk deep into the cushions. Sylvia had been gone for about an hour, and the waiting was unbearable. Neither of them wanted to look away, fearing the new roommate might arrive the moment they turned their backs.

The anticipation dragged on, cycling in Harriet's mind. She tried to distract herself, but it was futile. Thoughts of her chemistry lab next week snuck in, uninvited. Feeble attempts to hypothesize why the roommate hadn't shown up yet felt hollow. Maybe they'd gotten lost. Maybe they changed their mind. But none of it mattered. Tonight, one way or another, this would end.

Since Sylvia left, Harriet hadn't moved. Emberly hadn't stopped. She paced, paused to check the bay window, then started again. Harriet drifted further, her thoughts sliding sideways—out to the sidewalk, to the women laughing and drinking vodka from plastic bottles disguised as water.

Halloween.

Harriet had always liked the holiday, but never like other kids. While everyone else roamed the streets in costume, she stayed inside. Her mother's smothering paranoia kept her "safe." Safe from what? Razor blades in apples? LSD in candy? Harriet didn't know. But the fear stuck. They'd watch horror movies while her dad narrated the plot and she picked at candy her mother had pre-screened. She'd resented it. She'd resented them all.

Her classmates who screamed and sprinted through the neighborhood, laughter echoing into her room.

This time around she couldn't be more thrilled to be stuck inside where she was safe. Just like her mother wanted.

Now, she felt the same fear lodged in her stomach, the same restless longing for a normal night. A night where she didn't have to welcome a murderer to their home or hope a new roommate wouldn't stumble onto something she couldn't unsee. She blinked at the street outside, her eyes following a group in mismatched costumes. Cosplayers heading to a bar, no doubt. Others were dressed provocatively, bound for fraternity houses and clubs.

"What are you looking at?" Emberly's voice cut through the silence.

"Nothing," Harriet said, her voice faint. There was no way she could play dumb; she could feel the beads of sweat already forming just thinking about it.

Emberly sighed and moved toward the kitchen. "This is taking too long."

"You think she's okay?" Harriet asked.

"She'll be fine." Emberly's tone was clipped, but Harriet didn't believe her.

The unease lodged in Harriet's gut tightened. She didn't want to admit it—not out loud—but Sylvia's absence weighed on her.

If something went wrong tonight, there was no undoing it.

Emberly might not see it, but Harriet did. They were already in deeper than they could crawl out.

***

Emberly grabbed a mug from the cabinet, pouring herself tea more for the distraction than for comfort. Her hands were steady, but she felt something sharp behind her ribs making her jaw clench. She hated not being in control, hated that she couldn't just fix this mess herself. If it were up to her, they wouldn't even be in this situation. She would've called her family's lawyers, let them clean it up. But it wasn't her call. Sylvia insisted on doing it her way, and Emberly could only stand by and wait.

Her skin turned gooseflesh as she leaned over the front door's threshold, peering into the dark street. If Sylvia didn't return soon, Emberly would lose her mind. Pacing didn't help. Counting seconds didn't help. Nothing helped.

Her mind wandered, uninvited, to Penelope. Collateral damage, Sylvia had called her. Emberly didn't care. Penelope's own parents barely cared—she'd seen it at Family Weekend. They'd droned on about her being "troubled" and "wild" while refilling their wine.

What would they say now?

Emberly's grip tightened on the counter. It didn't matter. Penelope was gone. What mattered was Sylvia.

Sylvia, who needed her. Sylvia, who had *chosen* her. Not Edith.

She recalled the night they killed her—how Sylvia had looked at her afterward. The closure. The relief. That's all Emberly needed.

She glanced at Harriet, still catatonic on the couch. Emberly didn't care what Harriet was thinking. Sylvia's plan would work. *Right?* Sylvia's survival was important, but so was *her's*.

If she needed her again, Emberly would be there. No questions.

Always.

***

Emberly poured a second cup and set it on the table beside Harriet. She didn't speak. Neither did Harriet. The silence was unbearable—but somehow safer than trying to fill it.

Time dragged. Emberly leaned against the counter, her eyes flicking between the clock and the bay window. She didn't pray, but if she did, she would've prayed for Sylvia to come back soon—and for this to end.

CHAPTER THIRTY-THREE

Sylvia

Old tractors and rusting dump trucks littered the clearing, their hulking shapes casting jagged shadows under the moon. After fifteen minutes of searching, I found a soft patch of ground. My boots sank slightly in the loamy soil.

Good enough.

I pulled on gloves and took a long swig from my water bottle. My hands trembled as I picked up the shovel.

I hadn't even started digging and I was already sweating.

The first few swings were easy—the shovel bit into the forgiving earth. But my mind was racing. How long would this take? Hours? Would two be enough? Three? What if they weren't ready when I came back?

The world began to narrow to a pinpoint.

Just dig, I told myself.

I focused on the rhythm. Scoop, toss. Scoop, toss. The thud of dirt hitting the mound beside me was almost enough to quiet my thoughts.

Almost.

Two hours in, I was only two feet deep. The topsoil had been kind. Now I was hitting red clay—dense, compacted, and dry as stone. Every strike rattled my bones.

Sweat trickled down my temple, mixing with the dirt smeared across my skin. I wiped my forehead with the back of my glove and took a step back, leaning on the shovel for support. My head spun, and my stomach growled in protest. I regretted skipping dinner—hell, skipping every meal that day.

I pricked my ears at the sudden snap of a branch.

My head whipped around.

I grabbed my flashlight from the ground, my hands trembling as I clicked it on. The beam wavered through the trees, casting long shadows that seemed to move. My breath hitched when I caught a glint of reflective eyes in the darkness.

A deer.

My chest deflated in relief, but the tension didn't leave my body. The cold sweat clinging to my neck sent shivers down my spine, and no matter how hard I tried, I couldn't shake the feeling of being watched.

I turned back to the hole. Gripped the shovel tighter. *Just the deer,* I whispered. Like saying it aloud made it true.

I dug. I thought about Penelope. Hating her for being hurtful rather than fucking helpful. And do I really need to dig six feet?

I remembered one of those nights where she was a real pain in my ass like tonight. An Anything But Clothes party at Beta something or other. Pen had drunk too much, as usual. By the time we left, she was slumped in the back seat, too far gone to move.

I could still feel the weight of the grocery bag I'd held around Pen's face, just in case she puked. Emberly had driven, calm and composed, as always. I had sat behind her, half-asleep, until Pen turned to tell me something and vomited all over my lap.

We'd barely made it home. Emberly and I had tried to drag Pen up the stairs, but she was dead weight. I'd run back into the house, grabbed a mattress topper, and laughed deliriously as we slid Pen onto it.

"On three," I had said. "We taco the bitch. One. Two. Three."

We'd hoisted her up and gotten halfway to the door before Penelope puked on me again. I'd wanted to let her fall down the steps, and eventually, we did. It was only three steps, but it felt like karma.

We collapsed in the kitchen, laughing until our stomachs ached. It was messy. Raw. Real.

Now? That version of Penelope was gone. Replaced by a body in our living room, wrapped in plastic.

Three hours in. The grave was five feet deep.

I climbed out, legs shaking, arms screaming. I collapsed to my knees, gasping like I'd broken the surface of water.

"Good enough," I muttered.

I planted the shovel in the dirt and looked up.

My flashlight had rolled a few feet away. Its beam cast crooked shadows.

I crawled toward it, fingers closing around the handle—and I froze.

And froze.
The light swept toward the tree line.
A pair of feet.
Wide stance.
Still.
My breath caught. I adjusted the light slowly.
The beam rose, illuminating the silhouette.
They didn't move.
They just watched.

Chapter Thirty-Four

The living room felt smaller now, as if the air had thickened with dread. Harriet sat stiff in the armchair, fingers locked around the armrests. Emberly paced, her boots striking the floor in a steady, hostile rhythm.

"Where *is* she?!" Emberly snapped, her voice cutting through the silence like glass.

"Who?" Harriet asked quietly, not looking up.

"Fucking Sylvia, Harriet. Who else?" Emberly spun on her heel and glared. "She should be back by now."

"The new roommate hasn't shown up either," Harriet murmured, her voice distant.

"I don't care about the roommate! It's been, what— four hours? We had a plan. Sylvia was *supposed* to be back."

Storming out the front screen door, stepping onto the porch, Emberly scanned the trail in both directions, her head turning in quick, frantic movements, but there was no sign of Sylvia.

Circling to the corner of their street, Emberly caught sight of a public safety officer's car rolling past. The officer inside looked her way. She quickly averted her gaze, her heartbeat hammering in her ears. She forced herself to walk casually back to the house, entering through the back door.

"Nothing," she announced, her frustration boiling over.

Harriet spoke again, her voice too low for Emberly to catch.

"What did you say, Harry?"

"I asked if I should make tea," Harriet repeated softly.

Emberly groaned, running a hand through her hair. "No, Harry. *Focus.*" She resumed pacing, boots scuffing the hardwood. "Where the hell is Sylvia?"

"What if the cops already have her?" Harriet asked, her voice trembling.

"If they had her, they'd have all of us by now," Emberly said, too sharply. She winced at her own tone but didn't take it back.

Harriet just nodded, lips pressed in a pale line.

With a sigh, Emberly perched on the armrest of Harriet's chair and slipped an arm around her. "It's going to be okay, Harry. She'll come back."

"You don't know that."

"She's stubborn," Emberly said, more to herself. "But she's smart. She wouldn't do this unless she thought she could pull it off. Even if something went wrong... what's the worst? Trespassing? She'd talk her way out of it."

Harriet's head tilted, resting lightly against Emberly's arm. "I hope you're right."

***

Emberly pulled away, standing suddenly. "When do the RAs usually do inspections again?"

Harriet frowned, clearly calculating. "We're always last since we're so far off campus."

"How much time do we have?" Emberly asked, her voice rising.

"An hour, maybe less," Harriet answered.

"What if they inspect the basement?" Emberly demanded, her voice sharp.

Harriet's frown deepened. "Last year, they just wiggled the handle and didn't bother."

"But that doesn't mean they'll do the same thing now!" Emberly's frustration bubbled over as she threw her hands up.

"No," Harriet admitted softly, looking down at her lap. "It doesn't."

Chapter Thirty-Five

Sylvia

I didn't think—I just ran. My legs stumbled over rocks and roots, clumsy and frantic, but I didn't care how I looked.

What the hell was that?!

My pulse roared in my ears, drowning out everything. I clutched the key fob in my slick palm and hit unlock. Only the driver's side clicked. Good. Less risk.

I didn't see them coming.

A blur slammed into the side of the car. I hit the dirt hard, shoulder-first, pain radiating down to my fingertips. My skull buzzed, ears ringing.

I screamed.

Scrambling on hands and knees, I tried to crawl under the car. If I could just—

Something grabbed my ankle and yanked. I hit the ground, air knocked from my lungs.

"Let go of me!" I shrieked, thrashing, kicking. Useless.

They didn't let go.

I tried to rise, but they were on top of me, pressing me into the dirt, their weight anchored on my back. I kicked harder, but couldn't find leverage.

"Who the fuck *are* you?!" My voice tore from my throat.

Leather gloves clamped around my wrists. Their grip burned against my skin.

They know. They have to know who I am, what I was doing. But how?!

I thrashed, trying to roll, but their legs locked around mine, pinning me.

"Get off me!"

One arm broke free. I reached blindly and found my flashlight. I swung it upward, aiming for their head.

They grabbed my burned wrist.

The pain was white-hot. I screamed again.

The flashlight beam jittered across the clearing—and landed on their face.

Time stuttered, so did I.

No.

I knew that face.

"No," I whispered.

My whole body went limp.

Edith Aldridge.

She pried the flashlight from my hand like it was nothing. Her smirk twisted her mouth.

"Silly Syl," she said, voice soft. Like nothing had changed.

I tried to scream. To move. To *do* something.

She was dead. She *is* dead.

Sealed in duct tape.

I'd seen her die. I'd felt the blood, I thought, as the world went black.

Chapter Thirty-Six

My breath caught in my throat, followed by a giggle of triumph. Halloween. What a *perfect* night. And finally—Syl was mine.

Her body. Her breath. Her everything.

Everything I'd poured into the years between us—into a connection that had spanned nearly our entire lives—curdled into a low, aching hunger.

I could eat her to pieces now. But I needed time.

It's like that marshmallow test they do with kids where they have put a marshmallow out in front of them and are told they could eat it now or wait for a reward if they choose not to eat it after a specific time. The silly children who chose instant gratification were stunned when they saw the kids who waited get an additional marshmallow to eat at the end. The impotent, stupid kids that only got one would cry and beg and be in full tantrums when, to their dismay, they never actually got another one in the end. No matter how much they tried.

I had been so patient, waiting, watching. Longed to be close to her, stopping myself was a torture that never ended. At a certain point, I thought I would never get what

I wanted. It could be thirty years before the time was *right*.

I believed in Syl all along. Their whole lives, I trusted her to be herself. After all the high school years and lackluster confession, I knew Syl needed some time. Syl was never a murderer, but I would kill to be the center of her attention.

And look where it got you.

I kneeled to open my backpack, grabbed the rope, and began my fireman's chair knot. The rope was long, and when it was finished, I started dragging her toward the excavator. Syl's body was lighter than I anticipated.

All that stress never does the body *any* good, Syl.

Her limp body was positioned in the middle of the bucket and the tracks. I threw the rest of the length over the boom and pulled with my entire strength. I felt the tension and looked back. Syl was floating, her arms and legs dangling above me.

Perfect.

With the ropes taut in my hands, I stepped toward Syl and tied the final knot, sealing the diamond across her torso. It was even better than I imagined.

Watching her dangle—loosened, obedient, mine— filled me with a kind of pleasure I hadn't known I was capable of.

Men crave control. But women—women ache for power. Not in the same way. Ours is older. Quieter. Born from centuries of being cornered and told to smile through it.

So what happens when a woman takes what men are told they're entitled to? Power. Control. Ownership.

What then?

Maybe that's what scared her.

The hunger in me.

The way I clung to power like it could keep her close.

Syl never really saw me—not beyond what she needed me to be.

I don't think I saw myself either—not really—until she left.

It didn't hit right away. Not until I realized it wasn't men keeping us apart.

It was her. Her dithering. Her refusal to be pinned down.

And it was me—playing a role that was never mine.

That truth cracked something open.

And from the pieces, I built something new.

I changed.

After Syl's parents died and in her grief moved away, I sold my car with no need for it. Even if I did, I would just use my mother's. This part of me I suppressed for years grew into something I couldn't control, it was the forefront of everything that I knew made me unlovable. If Syl would have let me love her, I would have. She didn't see that I had all the qualities she looked for in the perfect partner. When I saw her posing with friends in the arts district in her college town, I knew I couldn't stay away. There were so many questions as to who these people were and why they had become more important than I.

A feeling was stirring in my gut I couldn't shake. It would move across my diaphragm and up into my chest not quite reaching my throat. I would stay up at night choking myself to sleep to force it away. You might say it's the dark identity that sat idly waiting for its chance to show its face to the world. Just when I would think it was gone for good it would reach out from the void and stroke my hair. Like a pet, coaxing me to become docile and pliant.

When I fed it scraps and watched Sylvia's family crumble and turn into shambles, I could hear this figure lurking in the dark chuckle. When I unlocked the sanctuary of my mind I lost it somewhere in the stacks and now it knows everything I tried to be. It showed me what wasted potential looked like for those who never acted on their darkest desires.

It wasn't the men in Sylvia's life that wanted to destroy her, but me. I wanted to be her. I wanted to fuck her. It's true that I couldn't face rejection. I would have destroyed every man in my path, but Sylvia was getting in the way of any semblance of progress. I'm a goal oriented person, and when I realized there was no goal to begin with and my time was wasted. The bitch didn't need to live.

Tightening the knots on her limbs sent a thrill up my spine. The more she struggled, the deeper they'd cut. I wanted her to wake up sore, her joints screaming the way my heart had for years.

This wasn't just about making her pay for my suffering.

This was about proving that I was never pathetic.

Never delusional.

I gave her hips a firm shake, feeling her muscles shift under my palms.

"Time to wake up, Syl," I whispered, right before she stirred.

Chapter Thirty-Seven

Edith stood behind Syl as she woke, startled and thrashing in her restraints.

"Hey! What the fuck is this? Let me go!"

"Now, why would I do that, Syl?"

Sylvia's head jerked up, her eyes widening as realization crashed over her.

"No."

Edith slithered into view, her voice coiled with venom. "Yes. It's me, Syl."

Sylvia could barely make out her eyes—but whatever looked back at her wasn't Edith. It was something grotesque, warped into a version that only resembled her. They stood in silence, and every second tightened around Sylvia's ribs like a noose.

"This is where I die, isn't it."

"Yessss. It is."

Edith laughed, and Sylvia writhed, yanking at the restraints in a panic she could no longer suppress.

"No. Nooo, noooooo, NOOOOO!"

"You picked a great spot, Syl. No one's going to hear you out here. You sound like a mating fox—I can't wait to see what else lies inside you. After all this time, it's so worth it."

"All this time?" Sylvia's voice cracked as she forced the words out. "How long?"

"Long enough to see what you've been up to since moving to college. I couldn't very well let you go off on your own." Edith puffed out her bottom lip in a mocking pout. "I was worried about you."

Sylvia thrashed harder now, not to escape—but to kill. "You fucking bitch!"

"I'm only kidding, Silly Syl. I was hoping I could come out to you again, profess my love, so you could squash my heart and lie to me. Again."

"I never fucking lied to you."

Edith began circling her, slow and deliberate, hands clasped behind her back.

"Did you or did you not tell me you were straight?"

Through gritted teeth: "Yes."

"Did you or did you not start dating another woman when you came to Discordia?"

"Yes."

"So, you're not straight."

"Yes. I am."

Edith reached behind her head and pulled out the machete. "See, that's where you're wrong, Syl. You're not. Are you lying to Em, too?"

"Yes."

"God. You're more fucking shallow than I thought." She wagged the machete toward Sylvia. "You're *good.*"

Tears poured down Sylvia's face as Edith kept going.

"I don't think it's us you're lying to, Syl. It's yourself.

Why are you always letting stupid men get between you and your soulmate? You're stuck in this hell-loop you create for yourself—won't be happy unless you're miserable. Good to see some things never change."

Sylvia spit in her direction, hitting her square on the forehead.

To her horror, Edith wiped it with a single finger and popped it into her mouth.

"You're fucking disgusting."

"Oh, *please*. You're so fucking sanctimonious. Who made you goddamn judge and jury? "

Edith stepped directly beneath her, their faces inches apart, her eyes cold and unyielding.

"I see you, Syl. And you're disgusting. Your fake righteousness, your illusions of superiority—steering you into the same pit, again and again. I didn't want it to be like this. I really didn't. If you hadn't let men—or excuse me, your repressed sexuality—get in the way... you would've seen it. We're the same, Syl. Two sides of the same coin. But now you die knowing you're no better than the person you tried to condemn. You're wasted potential. Not even worth saving at this point."

Shaking now. "How are you even alive?"

"You know, I thought you'd see through it. Instantly. But no—your vanity's too thick. You didn't even clock a well-made costume and a lookalike." Edith chuckled, amused by her own elaborate deception. "...Didn't expect you to kill her, though."

Tears mixed with snot, Sylvia's face twisted. "You killed my parents! What did you think I'd do? No one was doing anything—I had to!"

"You may have proof I was... obsessive. But really, Syl, what *actual* evidence do you have?"

"You stalked me!"

"Not a crime. Not murder."

Syl's head fell forward in defeat. Words dried up. She hated how right Edith was. How easy it was to see herself, a little drunk, surrounded by friends who always nodded, never challenged her.

"I have horrible friends."

"Oof. Hate that it took all *this* for you to realize you're the problem."

"Just tell me. Did you kill them or not? I need to know."

Edith laughed, the kind that comes when someone breaks.

"I don't know—you seem to have all the answers. You tell me, Syl. *Did I?*"

"FUCK! EDITH, STOP! JUST FUCKING TELL ME!"

Sylvia twisted violently, the restraints biting into her skin.

"You can thank your... whatever-she-is for the bondage lessons. Watching her make you a whimpering simp behind closed doors was—"

"You sick fuck," Sylvia hissed.

"Maybe."

Then Edith turned and walked off, vanishing around a bend.

Sylvia's heart pounded too loud to hear her footsteps. In a burst of futile bravado, she shouted after her:

"I *know* it was you! Edith! *EDITH!*"

Only the silence responded to her.

When Edith came back, she gazed at her design. If her arms were outstretched, Edith would compare Sylvia to Jesus in *The Crucifixion* by Fra Angelico. Lifeless, but a soul still existed, their aura emanating defeat and hope simultaneously. Edith put a hand to her chest and rubbed in a circle moving whatever feeling was mustering in her chest to be spread elsewhere to dissipate. She could cry tears of joy watching her masterpiece come to fruition.

Beautiful.

Syl recoiled at her touch, and Edith tutted. "Such a shame. I wanted to watch you grow old."

"Funny. I thought you wanted me dead."

"Oh, I do. But first we talk. Closure, or whatever. You *need* to know who I am."

"Oh, I fucking *know* who you are," Sylvia sneered.

Edith stepped into full view and gestured. "Go on."

"You're jealous of me."

Edith scoffed.

"You always have been. You hated everything I did. Snickered at my popularity in high school, and I *still* loved you. Even when I got a boyfriend, you were either lurking behind us or trying to get in his head—convince him I wasn't enough. Not for him. Not for anyone. Only for *you*.

"All those opportunities you made me second guess? That was all just so you could keep me close. Stuff me up your cunt and pretend you gave birth to me. You slithered into all the cracks in my life and cemented yourself there. I couldn't get rid of you. All you wanted was my body, my mind, my *soul*. Who the *fuck* does that?"

"Me."

"Exactly. *You.* No one else is this fucking twisted. You murdered my *family*. And see, the thing is, I wasn't alone in trying to kill you. I didn't even have to say much to convince others that you deserve to die. They thought it was the most reasonable reaction I could have had. Even if that's a lie, I know the truth. I don't care what anyone says. Like, who the fuck goes to this extent, all because I wouldn't put out for you? Because I didn't want to sit at home and look at your *fugly* face for the rest of my life?! I know who you are Edith, you're fucking sick in the head. You're a psychopath that I should have never, *ever,* befriended."

Edith looked on, appearing to contemplate, "Are you done?"

Sylvia started wailing and screaming. Non-stop for three minutes. Even made the bats in the trees swarm around them and away. "Great. You scared all the wildlife."

Syl's thrashing began to slow. Defeated. Resigned.

"Just let me go," she whispered. "We've both done horrible things, but we can still live. Just let me go. Please. I'll do anything."

"There's nothing left I want from you." Edith crossed her arms and looked away like a sullen child.

"Edie… I know you're still in there. Somewhere. Despite *everything,* I believe there's still love in your heart for me. There *has* to be. There has to be something I can do. Just tell me what it is… and I'll do it."

CHAPTER THIRTY-EIGHT

Before

Finding a double wasn't easy given the time frame I had. I spent nights at dilapidated rest stops, scouting lot lizards no one would ever miss. All they needed was a willingness to wear a light amount of prosthetics, and they'd get half the money upfront. It was wild how many of these women trusted greasy men with pot bellies so big they couldn't see their own dicks, but hesitated when a woman offered them good money to play pretend.

After days of dead ends, I finally found the hook when one of them told me, "They always get us McDoubles when it's overnight."

I leaned over my passenger seat and offered my hand. "Edith."

She skipped the handshake and got in, tossing her tote bag into her lap. "I'm Hannah."

I turned the ignition and pulled out onto the road. First stop: McDonald's.

After inhaling six burgers, Hannah was finally willing to listen.

"So look," I said, "all you have to do is live with me for a bit, learn about my life, and act as a stand-in. You in?"

Mouth full of a seventh McDouble, she nodded.

Thank you to the makeup artist at Sephora for the flawless no-makeup look, and the cosmetologist who nailed the exact hair color match. When my mother died and I inherited the house, it was easy to bring a stranger in—and honestly, kind of nice to have company. As long as she cleaned, I fed her and gave her an allowance until the big debut.

Hannah called me "Mother" when I made her a real meal and we sat at the table, eating while I lectured her on all the lore—even the bad parts. It became something like a confessional. I didn't try to stop the anxious attachment curling around us; I'd been alone too long.

In time, she told me no one had really cared for her. Not since she was a baby.

Talking to someone who wasn't Sylvia about personal matters was like taking a scalpel to my arm and someone took tweezers finding the nerve and snipping it making me bleed out. It was an intense couple of months. The sessions were religious and daily. Hannah learned the ins and outs of what life was like as Sylvia's punching bag, all the way through the death of her parents, the rejection, and bittersweet end to our friendship that followed.

One afternoon, Hannah asked, "Why would you keep trying to be friends with her anyway? She sounds like a bitch."

"That's exactly why. She always got what she wanted."

"I don't know… this is getting kind of weird. If she knows you that well, won't she clock me the second she sees me?"

I slammed my fists on the table, making her flinch and shrink into her seat. Towering over her, I snapped, "It's been years!"

I sat down again, raising my hands in surrender. "I know it sounds insane. But I've written her every week since she left. No replies. And now that she has—now that there's a thread—I'm scared. I just want to see what happens."

Her voice was small. "But she's your friend. If you were writing to her, wouldn't you want to see her instead? Get closure?"

I folded my arms on the table. "Look. Stop asking questions. If this doesn't work—which it won't—she'll just kick you out and think I'm still the weirdo I've always been."

Walking on eggshells, Hannah muttered, "Okay. But how do you—"

I cut her off. "What did I just fucking say?"

"I get it. But I'm gonna have questions if I'm the one going. I mean… if it's been years, isn't it weird she'd invite a 'long-lost friend' she was grossed out by?"

"Okay, harsh. But I think she knows I have my flaws, right? To your point, she wouldn't have reached out unless she was ready for me. She wants closure and I'm not against it. That's just her MO. In high school, she would cry for days over someone she dated for less than a week because she always needed a way to bring the story to a close. Trust me, surface level everything is best anyways considering the circumstance. Just be you, well, you're rendition of me. She reached out already, she's expecting me, and we have a limited amount of time. Either way, you have no choice."

"I'm just worried that she didn't invite you to make amends. What if she wants to, I don't know, like beat you up or something?"

I reached out, giving a soft double tap on Hannah's shoulder. "It will be fine."

***

I've made plenty of resource documents and recordings of my voice for her to practice cadence. There should be plenty to occupy. "I'll be back. Don't get into trouble."

Since she moved in, it's been cathartic. I bought frozen

cheeseburgers and fries from Costco. I figured she'd be satisfied while continuing her education.

"Anything else, Mother dearest?" she teased.

Climbing into my car, I couldn't help but laugh. The best prisoners are the ones who don't realize they're imprisoned. I locked the door, started the engine, and headed toward Discordia for reconnaissance.

Since she left, I still popped in—just to keep an eye on her.

She lived too far for it to be regular, and I had my own studies to manage. But over the last few weeks, I became a full-time voyeur in Sylvia's life.

Old habits really do die hard.

I knew her schedule by heart.

And her hobbies?

Cheating on her girlfriend. Sneaking around with some frat guy who gets her into exclusive parties.

Once, I tried to warn her—she was playing with fire. But I thought she'd understand the message without me having to spell it out.

The guy probably had a fiancée back in Boston, waiting to settle down after grad school.

He asked for her number at a back-to-school party. She played coy.

When they met at a bar, just the two of them, I couldn't resist.

I sent her favorite cocktail. Anonymously.

Wore a brunette wig to match the description I knew she'd be given.

Left before the drink even reached her.

Then watched from across the street as she squirmed, scanning the room in panic.

The bartender gave a vague description—dark hair, angular

face, intense eyes. To anyone else, meaningless. To Sylvia? It was her girlfriend.

Later that night, I watched them fight—loud enough I swear I could hear it from a hundred yards away.

I imagine she pulled out the crocodile tears, mixed with whatever bile-coated fears she could wrench from her gut.

By the end of it, I'd bet money Emberly was the one apologizing—blaming herself for putting Sylvia in a position to cheat.

But of course, it ended in aggressive makeup sex.

Damn.

You have to be a pro to twist everything like that.

Syl was a master at making it anyone's fault but her own.

I should've expected it.

I had to yank out a chunk of my hair just to calm down.

It took three hours for the light in her room to finally go out.

I left. Wandered the campus aimlessly, mind racing. So much could go wrong. If I slipped up—if Hannah slipped up—it would all collapse. My investment in her would be a total loss.

I was risking real pain.

But I needed to know what she thought of me.

Sometimes, I'd manufacture stress. Steal her keys from the student center while she was in the bathroom. Move her bag to another booth. I once stole a package from her doorstep—just boots. Not her style, anyway.

Sometimes she'd leave her student ID on a table. I'd pick it up, return it later—outside her door, or on a walking path I knew she'd take. Right place, right time.

Of course I made a spare key. Thank you, carefree college girls. But mostly… I just liked watching her come undone.

Now, watching Sylvia stroll through her flat without a care in the world, I barely recognize her. She's not the girl I fell in love with. Still, I couldn't let go of the compulsion to be near her.

Do you know what it's like to watch someone for years and never be able to touch them?

Do you know the exact scent of their hair and laundry?

It's torture.

And at some point, I started to feel it—I deserved a reward. It buzzed on my skin like static. Surged through me like electricity.

The anticipation almost killed me.

Watching "me" pretend to be me should've been the cruelest part. But instead, it gave me hope. That Hannah might be the final piece.

And that maybe—finally—this would give me closure as well.

I remembered our last sleepover. I could taste her on my tongue. Her hormones were probably flooding when I inhaled the top of her head, the crook of her neck. She was succulent then, and I would bet she still is. Her white tea, lilac shampoo, and other floral qualities I couldn't pinpoint. It all became too much.

Once they all went to the cafe to have dinner together. I used my spare to go in, knowing exactly where Sylvia rested her head at night.

I had to know if she still smelled the same.

Leaning down to inhale her scent from the pillow, I detected it wasn't quite the same. Her immune system mixed with her girlfriend's. Satisfied to have an answer, I turned to leave and could have sworn I noticed a shadow figure move out from the corner of my eye.

Must have been paranoia.

After pausing, covering my breath, I heard nothing. Fleeing the room, I descended two stairs at a time, and checking the walkway before I left.

It was cocky of me, but I needed something to hold me over. When I saw the coast was clear, I returned to my sanctuary behind the mausoleums near Mother's Acre.

Behind the trees, I caught my breath. I didn't care how reckless it was. It was the most exhilarating thing I'd done since the last time I slept in her bed.

Sylvia thinks she's hardened by pain, but she's been behind glass this whole time—in a house I built. And she has no idea.

Maybe it doesn't matter if Hannah blows her cover.

Because either way—I'll find another method to break Sylvia apart and put her back together.

As many times as I want.

Whether she likes it or not.

Chapter Thirty-Nine

Each moment that passed had to feel like an eternity to Sylvia. She might've felt clueless a thousand times before, but right now, nothing mattered more than survival. "Edie…" she whimpered into the darkness.

Edith continued pacing behind her, silent, as Sylvia pissed herself. The fear in her eyes was a pathetic ruse she couldn't hide anymore—not from her.

"Come on! Edie, this is dramatic, don't you think?"

"I want you to admit your part in your parents' death."

Sylvia's chest heaved as she spat at Edith. "Fuck. You."

She kept thrashing with no success. Writhing like a butterfly trapped in its cocoon.

"Edie, come on—we can work this out. I didn't mean to—"

That's when Edith finally stepped into full view.

"Didn't mean to what? Kill me? I don't know, Syl—kidnap and torture sounds pretty intentional."

"You killed my parents! Again, *what* was I supposed to *do*?" Sylvia wailed. "They didn't deserve to die like that."

Edith circled slowly, drinking in the sight of Sylvia on display. "They died because your dad wasn't who you thought he was. Not to mention how you and your complacent mother enabled it."

"No! Look—you killed them, and yeah, I tried to kill you for it! Just let me go and we can call it even. I swear to God."

Edith chuckled, silent for a beat as Sylvia continued.

"You've always been jealous of me! Jealous that I had better parents than you! Can you not admit *that*?! Come on, Edie—don't be immature. Get real with yourself. Who does this shit besides a psychopath who *killed my parents?*"

Sylvia could have sworn she heard her father's voice in her head: *No begging. Always negotiate.* She forced her breathing to slow.

Edith finally responded.

"Your dad would be so proud of you."

"Don't you fucking *dare*," Sylvia spat. "For the love of God, just tell me the truth. Did you kill my parents, Edith? I *have* to know. Please! Tell me, and we can move on. I won't say anything—if you don't."

Edith slowly turned to meet Sylvia's eyes. She shrugged with a deadened indifference. "Does it matter?"

Sylvia screamed, "You don't want to do this!" just as she braced herself for the blow.

To her surprise, Edith swung the machete—cutting the rope that held her, but not the bindings. Sylvia crashed to the ground with a deep, bone-jarring thud and gasped for breath.

Sylvia could have sworn she heard something crack. A stray piece of glass embedded into her elbows and her vision doubled.

Edith turned her over, facing her directly.

"We can get past this," she offered.

Sylvia blinked in disbelief, a wave of hope breaking over her. "Really?"

For a second, she thought this was the end—that she was free and the act was over.

"I just need to see what's in your heart, Syl."

Sylvia's head snapped up, eyes going wide—just as the squelching began.

She didn't comprehend what was happening as Edith took meat claws and stabbed into her chest like a smoked hog. Plunging just under the rib cage, she yanked outward, cracking everything open. Pulling out, she would stab back into the area, trying to dodge the heart but open everything around it. Blood splattered all over Edith's face and clothes as blood filled Sylvia's esophagus. A little got in her eye as she heard Sylvia barely choke out, "Edie… please…"

Those gargled choking sounds were something of Edith's fantasies as she licked the blood from her lips, savoring the iron, Sylvia's life-force flooding her mouth. Giggles escaped as she dropped the claws and thrust her hand into the mangled chest cavity. The wet, meaty suction of flesh and bone parting echoed into the night.

Sylvia tried to move. Her body refused.

She could feel the blood pooling beneath her, soaking into the dirt. Her breath stuttered—shallow, slower.

It wouldn't last.

Sylvia felt the warm hand of a shadow cup her cheek. Another smoothed her hair, careful and unhurried.

A warm hand cupped her cheek. Another smoothed her hair, careful and unhurried.

She recognized the touch before she opened her eyes.

Her father knelt beside her. His expression was calm. Patient. Proud.

He placed his hand on her shoulder.

"Care for a drive?" he asked softly.

She tried to answer. The words burned in her throat. *Yes. Are you proud of me?*

But nothing came. Her mouth opened—only blood bubbled out.

She choked.

All she heard was the wet rattle of her own breath as she faded into nothing.

When Edith plunged her fingers into Sylvia's corpse, she felt the heart just underneath her fingertips. She squeezed. Hard. Until it bulged between her fingers.

And yanked.

Even in the dim light, Edith could've sworn she saw a flicker of life in Sylvia's eyes—watching her.

Accusing her.

For good measure, she retrieved the machete from behind her back and swung it hard into Sylvia's face. Her body slumped. Her eyes darted, unfocused. Twitching.

"You'll always be mine," Edith whispered as she brought the heart to her mouth and bit deep into the left atrium. Chewed. Swallowed.

She wiped her blade clean on Sylvia's calf, then slipped it back into its sheath. Wiped her eyes. Smiled at her victory.

Eventually, the spasms stopped. The brain stopped

firing.

Sylvia was still.

But where had her soul gone?

Edith stared into the lifeless eyes. Sylvia had never looked more beautiful at that moment. She looked her best when she had nothing going on in that little brain of hers. Edith grabbed a stray piece of Sylvia's hair and put it behind her ears, "Beautiful."

Edith cut the bindings that remained. Looking at her body, lifeless, gave Edith a release that felt more euphoric than any orgasm she hoped Sylvia might once give. Having her soul in her hands, devouring her whole, Edith knew this was the best choice she could have made.

If asked to do it again, she would do it just to feel her heartbeat stutter under her palm. To feel it turn into a stress ball—pliable, dissolving. To see that flicker of terror in her eyes just as her nightmares became real.

"Divine," Edith breathed.

She tucked the heart into her backpack, grabbed Sylvia by the feet, and dragged her toward the grave.

Chapter Forty

I was never going to let her be free. Not really.

Not while I still had pieces of her—tangled in old memories, buried in my mouth like a secret.

She would always chase the next warm body, always look for some boy to tell her what she was worth.

And me? I would always tighten the grip.

That's how this ends. It was *always* going to end like this.

When I acted on impulse, things always seemed to fall into place, while Sylvia spent her life learning every lesson the hard way. She was so reactive, constantly bending to the whims of her surroundings. Syl was a flower—delicate, always fearful someone might uproot her from the soil she'd carefully chosen. But what Syl never understood was that *I* was the soil. And no matter how deeply she burrowed into me, I couldn't nourish her. I had nothing to give. Still, she clung tighter, her roots sinking into barren ground, blind to the truth: I wasn't where she'd bloom—I was where she'd rot.

I didn't fully commit to murdering Syl in the beginning. Part of me hoped she might redeem herself when I came out of the shadows. But she had already descended too far, and what she did—what she made others do to Hannah—was unforgivable. Something cracked and chipped in my ceramic heart when Syl rejected me. But it shattered when I saw her true intentions upon my arrival. Hannah had gone in my place, not knowing she was the sacrificial lamb. And honestly, it was hard to swallow that I could have been the one tortured and dead.

Eye for an eye, as they say.

I couldn't do anything. The relationship was irreparable by that point. I had no choice. A wounded dog. Unable to go on.

I mean, look how her life ended—killing the wrong person, an orphan surrounded by terrible friends, self-destructive to the core. She made impulsive decisions that only ever led her to one inevitable end.

I've killed three people, only one of them had time to beg.

I've yet to feel anything a regular human should feel when they watch a soul leave its vessel.

When I smelled Mrs. Harrington's perfume long after I'd left. When I made a small cut on her mother's scarred inner thigh, there was little to no pain when she made her slow descent within her dream realm. Nothing. It had to be simple and quick so that I could deal with her father.

At that point in the night, Sylvia was occupied but could have returned home at any minute, so either way, I had to work fast. I wanted to make a spectacle of him. The world needed to know he was a horrible husband that might not have killed his wife but made damn sure she didn't live a life worth having. I did her a favor. Trust me.

He was already dead to her, lying there with his back turned when he heard a noise downstairs. He saw the front door was ajar. Sticking his head out, he leaned his whole body into the frame—neckless, slow. Sighing with relief, he locked it shut. But when he turned around, he noticed muddy footprints leading down into the open basement.

He gulped audibly and detoured to the kitchen to grab a .45 caliber he kept in a stand mixer in the lower cabinet. He didn't realize it was empty when he headed towards the basement's threshold, finger-ready on the trigger. Taking a couple steps down to reach the light, Mr. Harrington could see the neon lights flickering and no apparent shadows. When he felt a light tap on his shoulder, he was stunned to find it was me.

I gave him a swift kick in the chest. It was hilarious as he tried to shoot his gun right between my nose. I got to see that little fleck of surprise, anger, and grief pass over his face when he heard the clicks of an empty gun. As he fell, I heard his temple smack on the bottom of the banister. He seized slightly as the blood pooled around his head. I felt nothing but joy.

It wasn't the most grand and spectacular version of how I thought things should go, but I was more satisfied I succeeded. Leaving the wife murdered as she was could be risky, but it wouldn't matter. I covered my tracks well enough; any DNA would have been from another time I'd been around. My presence was embedded in that house. All I had to do was stage a robbery.

I took everything valuable. Tried to pry open the safe. I didn't want to break it, but it had to look like someone tried. There was at least a quarter million worth of jewelry in the dresser. I had to make a mess. Couldn't look like I knew where to find it.

Downstairs, I dumped the junk drawers, scattered loose change, and smashed the television. Turned over furniture. Then I slipped out the back door and set the security system. Locking the door behind me, I picked a decent point of entry and smashed a window to sound the alarm. The siren screamed. Lights blazed. But her parents never had cameras—would've gotten in the way if they "handled things themselves."

In the dark, I ran into the woods. Waiting for police to show.

It was gratifying watching Sylvia pulled into the driveway.

Patting down the soil in this junkyard, I finally laid everything to rest. Blood dried across my face. The white button-down I wore for the occasion was so soaked it looked like a Blade movie extra.

Tossing the shovel aside, I dropped to my knees and began to say a few words.

"I didn't want it to be this way," I whispered, the words spilling from my chest. "If only you'd accepted me as I was… you would've realized we were two sides of the same coin. I loved you."

All I could think was how grateful Sylvia must have been for her friends' help. But she wasn't coming back.

From the passport and ticket in the glovebox, looks like she wasn't planning on returning either. I could picture her booking it in real time, telling herself she had no choice. After what she did, she couldn't go back.

Every killer gets caught eventually, better them than

her I guessed.

Drenched in Sylvia's blood, I didn't bother cleaning myself off. A single tear slipped from my left eye.

I had dedicated years of my life to another person.

And now that she was gone—what was there to live for?

Anything fucking else. Finally triumphant.

The game was over. And maybe, yeah… maybe I took it too far.

But it's like when someone says "kill yourself" and you actually do—whose fault is that?

It's both. It's neither.

Put two people in a room. Their patience is tested, and with a few bodies between them, you're bound to see the ugly parts of each other.

The tires scream as I take the ramp onto the interstate, the whole car shuddering under my grip. I shove the windows down, letting the wind claw at my skin, whipping my blood-crusted ponytail like a flag.

"Tom Tom" by Holy Fuck blasted through the speakers—so loud it rattled my ribs, so loud it drowned out the wild laughter bubbling up from my throat.

I could still feel it. The heat of the kill. The slick blood. The exact moment Sylvia's body stopped fighting.

I stuck my arm out the window, fingers spread, watching the wind drag streaks of blood down my wrist, thinned by the wet fog.

It didn't matter. I couldn't have given a single fuck, even if you paid me.

Let the evidence smear, fade—disappear into the night like it was never mine to begin with.

Nothing could ruin my fucking high.

Tonight, I'm going back where I belong.

I park across the street—not behind the Flats. Not *yet*. A queen doesn't return without an offering.

I sling my knapsack over one shoulder and cut through the night, boots smacking pavement. The cold fogs my breath, but inside—I'm burning.

As I pass Flat C, I glance up. Harriet's still as stone, expression unreadable. Emberly? Pacing like a caged animal, gnawing her nails.

They don't know.

Good.

By the time I reach the cemetery, the air has shifted. The wind dies. The leaves still. Even the frogs, the crickets, and the distant hum of traffic—gone.

It's like Discordia herself is watching.

Each step toward the grave feels louder.

The rub of my soles against brick—too sharp. Too deliberate. Like the world is forcing me to listen.

My pulse thrums in my ears.

I stop in front of the flat stone—the first professor of Discordia. The foundation.

Carefully, I unzip the bag. My fingers find it. Slick. Wet. Still warm.

I place the heart on the grave like a relic. A promise. A declaration.

The silence stretches, swallowing me whole.

And then—a shift. Subtle. Unmistakable.

Something in the air changes.

The night exhales.

And I do, too.

Now, I don't have to stay in the shadows anymore.
I belong here.

Chapter Forty-One

Hours had passed. Emberly was pacing, her phone clutched tightly in her white-knuckled grip, waiting for an update. She'd received an alert from the Residential Director about a delay due to a male visitor streaking across campus.

Biting her nails, she muttered, "Harry, what time is it? She's not back yet. She *promised* she would be back!"

"Almost two," Harry said quietly.

"Fuck!" Emberly ran her fingers through her hair and didn't bother fixing it.

Harriet, somehow, had subdued her panic. She buried herself in her studies, trying to appear normal, natural, detached.

Emberly paced again, eyes darting from the door. "Even the sluts are returning. What are we supposed to do? We *can't* just sit here!"

"Em, we have to stay put. Moving the bodies ourselves could sabotage Syl's plan."

"Goddammit, I'm so fucking antsy."

"Em."

"I'm losing my *mind*. I'm about to say 'fuck Sylvia's

plan' and make our own. We have to do something, or that basement gets searched and we hand them corpses wrapped like party favors."

"We have to trust—"

"*Fuck* trust! Trusting her might be our *death*, Harry. What then?"

"We have to. There's also a chance they won't check at all. It's late."

Growing more exasperated, Emberly snapped, "It's an all-women's campus on *Halloween*—and there's already been an incident. They *plan* for this shit. They don't want a lawsuit. They *will* check. You know we can't plan for *if*—it's *when*. Don't tell me you trust Sylvia. Don't be naive. For all we know, she could be out of the country already, and we're the idiots left holding the bag, thinking she was saving us when she was saving *herself*."

"You're projecting, and that's more hurtful than helpful right now, Emberly Stratton. Sit down and stick to the plan."

"I'll stick to the plan. But I *can't* sit." She glanced toward the kitchen. "Want another pot of tea?"

"That would make three, Emberly. I'm good."

"I'll make you another one anyway. Can't drink it alone."

Emberly's footsteps echoed as she disappeared into the kitchen. Harriet tried to zone out, the sound of the kettle clinking against the stovetop blending with the pages of her anatomy textbook.

"Should I set out a third cup for our *roommate*?" Emberly called.

Harriet peeked over the top of her book.

For a moment, she didn't register it—the hour, the silence, the no-show.

"No."

She glanced at the door, then the clock, still holding on. Maybe they'd come tomorrow.

It wasn't like inspections were tea socials. No one ever planned to stay.

As if on cue, the doorbell rang.

"Shit."

Emberly clanked her silverware. Even though it wasn't done, she poured hot water into cups with bags. She headed through the hallways and saw the campus police officer and Resident Director. Nodding and smiling, she said, "One second," gesturing to her teacups.

After setting them down next to Harriet, they both looked at each other knowingly, having a mental conversation in microseconds.

All Harriet could muster in the volume of a mouse, "The bodies."

"It's on me. She didn't make it. It's been nice knowing you." Emberly stood and walked toward the door without another glance.

Harriet kept her expression controlled. Thank God she was pale—no one could see the color drain from her face as Emberly twisted the knob.

She opened the door and flashed her best smile. "Hey there! Come on in!"

The Resident Director, Suma, looked exhausted and went straight to business. She tossed the end of her hijab over her shoulder and adjusted her posture, clipboard in hand.

"Anyone else home?" she asked, eyes scanning the main floor.

"Just us," Harriet replied. She let Emberly handle the talking. It was their norm.

"New flatmate settling in okay?"

"As far as we know, she hasn't shown up yet."

"Hm. Hopefully she shows by tomorrow. Let me know if you haven't heard from her by then, okay?"

They both nodded. Emberly offered a quick, "Sure."

They were shaking like leaves but thanked whatever god they had that they were the *last* inspection.

Harriet noticed the campus guard's glazed-over stare. He was checked out. Didn't care. No one was partying. No one was in costume. They looked like introverts with no plans—*perfect*.

"Alright! Let's do this thing," Suma said brightly. "Give me the grand tour. We'll start from the top."

She motioned them up the stairs. Harriet's pulse quickened. She couldn't grow eyes in the back of her head. She *hoped* the upper floor was spotless. They'd cleaned everything. The basement was the only problem.

If they could keep them from going down there, they could figure out what to do in the morning. Everyone would be hungover and wouldn't be up at six in the morning. They could pick up where she left off, except they had no idea where she fucking planned to dispose of them.

Ascending the stairs, Harriet thought how insane it was that Suma was trailing behind her and couldn't hear her thoughts. All she could think about was where *Sylvia* might be.

Did she plan to bury them? She wouldn't be brave enough to dismember. Harriet envisioned Sylvia as totally fine and on her way back, but a *big part* of her thought she was on a plane to another country, and she left them to take the fall when the RD inevitably came.

They started at the front and worked their way back. Emberly kept the chatting to a minimum, and Harriet let her vision go out of focus and sank into herself to stay safe while she tried to solve their problem.

Emberly went on about how blessed they were to have an extra room, furnished just in case a guest stayed overnight. She droned, all syrupy pride and verbal diarrhea.

It was open in Emberly and Sylvia's room, the mess was minimal. Some clothes missed the hamper. The rug was stained from months of wear.

Suma told the guard to sweep the room. He knelt, checking under furniture.

Trying to lean into her nerves, Harriet asked, "Any Boogeymen?"

The guard chuckled awkwardly. Unable to determine if she was serious. Hard to tell at this school.

They shut the bathroom window and didn't mention how much it smelled like bleach as they moved to Penelope's room. Emberly steadied her breath, mentally noting everything and how she dusted everything perfectly and left it just as she had. Harriet found it difficult to do anything and headed to the hall, gravitating towards the last room for Harriet and whoever was planning to move in.

The guard checked the final nook and cranny while

Suma took notes on their dorm sheet. Everyone's head peeped up when they heard the signature squeak and creak of the front door opening and shutting.

Harriet and Emberly's faces were panicked as they watched Suma peer over the railing and descend the stairs. Their hearts dropped as they listened for anything to signify that Sylvia had returned.

"Hi there! Welcome to your new home! Did you go to a party? Your costume is awesome! Very real looking!"

"Thank you! It's corn syrup. The trick is cocoa powder with the dye."

"I'll have to remember that! Glad you made it. We're just finishing dorm checks. Girls! Come meet your new flatmate!"

"One second!"

Emberly yanked Harriet into her room.

"It's over, Em. It's *over*. We're finished."

"No. Listen. Sylvia might not come back, but this girl has no idea what's going on."

Emberly tucked a strand of hair behind Harriet's ear. The lights flickered.

"Harry, breathe. It's okay. Let's get through the introductions, then deal with the basement."

The guard appeared. "Something in the basement?"

Harriet couldn't turn around. Her throat seized.

Emberly jumped in. "No! She meant *debasement*. You touched her figurines. Be more careful."

He rolled his eyes and left.

They had to follow. No choice.

When they reached the living room, everything slowed.

The new girl turned around.

And they saw her.

Edith.

A tight-lipped grin became a full-tooth smile.

"Hi, I'm Edith. Sorry I'm so late."

They were speechless.

Suma said, "Girls, you look like you've seen a ghost. Don't be rude, introduce yourselves!"

It was true. They were looking at a ghost. There should be no reason that Edith had risen from the dead to return as a flatmate, covered in blood. There was nothing artificial about it. Yet, she stood, head tilted down with her eyes fixed on us, giddy.

Harriet felt nothing but dread. Neither Emberly nor Harriet had ever experienced this level of confusion. Either Edith was a ghost, and they all had enough lack of sleep to start hallucinating, or she rose from the fucking grave to be their new flatmate. Harriet was frozen as Emberly peered into her eyes to see that it looked like Edith, even smelled like the Edith they met, and she was covered in blood that was not hers. Not a scratch or bruise from the wreckage she bore on her body.

"GIRLS!" Suma yelled, startling both of them.

"I'm Emberly."

"Harriet."

Edith stood up straight and returned to appearing human when everyone looked for her response. She threw her arm out to shake their hands. "It's a pleasure to meet you. I can't wait to settle in," she said, smiling but completely detached.

They didn't extend their hands to return the shake.

"GIRLS!"

On command, they both offered their hands simultaneously, but Emberly reached in first, and death gripped Edith's hand to check if she was real, "Pleasure is mine."

Edith didn't flinch as Emberly rubbed her knuckles together. Harriet gave a limp shake, barely touching her skin, and nodded. Stepping back immediately to create some distance between them.

They couldn't predict what would follow. Filling the awkward silence, Edith began talking with her hands, "Wow, I love this space; the wood floors are solid. So what's on that floor beneath us? Do people live there?"

Emberly felt her heart drop to her asshole, and Harriet was stunned, but you couldn't tell the difference because she had been that flustered the entire time.

Suma answered, "God no! It was once an apartment but is now a dirty, gutted basement with no floors. It's unlivable; otherwise, it's empty besides the circuit breaker." The guard gave a nod, confirming.

The blood began trickling into Edith's mouth. She didn't wipe it.

"Yeah, sounds scary. Any squatters?"

"Heavens no!" Suma waved it off. "Well… we did have a peeping tom once. But not down there."

Turning to the guard, "Let's go ahead and check it just to be safe."

Suma headed to the back. Emberly bolted ahead, arms spread to block the door.

"Step aside," the guard ordered.

She didn't move.

"Emberly, please," Suma said.

"It's locked. No one's down there. We haven't heard a peep, have we, Harriet?"

Everyone turned to Harriet, making herself as small as possible in the corner. Harriet knew the look on Emberly's face could mean one thing. She was about to be wrapped in a situation her family lawyer couldn't get her out of. Harriet was a woman of logic, and the probability of this ending well was nothing.

No one would save them. Nothing would change their minds.

They had to check.

Harriet only shrugged, words failing her as she glanced at Edith—still grinning, all teeth and murder.

There were too many moving parts to this, and so much was uncertain. Harriet crumbled under the highest probable outcome of all her choices.

"I don't know what's happening, but we must check. If you have drugs or something, tell us now." Suma glanced sideways at the guard, who appeared to feel the breeze flowing through their ears. "Since it's Halloween, I get it, people like to do stupid shit. But, you have to tell us now."

Emberly looked frantically between Harriet and Suma. Edith hadn't changed her expression but tilted her head like a curious canine as Emberly declared, "Yeah! There's weed in there; I stashed it there—no need to go down. I'll retrieve it now, and you can confiscate it. Can we call this a deal?" She delivered with astounding grace, leaning in while shrugging and raising her eyebrows like a car salesman.

Suma responded, "Well, thank you for your honesty, but I still have to go search it since you confirmed it's in there." Since she fell from the doorframe, Suma could gently nudge her aside while she made her way to the back stairs.

Emberly was breathing down her neck, pleading, "Please, Suma. Come on, let's work something out. It's a mess down there."

"I'm sorry, Emberly, but I have to follow protocol. Bill, do you have the ghost key?"

"Sure do." He looked smug. You could tell this place hardly gets any action if the prospect of finding a little weed enticed him.

Harriet stayed behind, her feet planted, frozen in place. Waiting to hear them finish going down the stairs and deal with Emberly, who attempted to block the basement threshold, Edith looked over to Harriet.

It's hard to explain what being under a gaze like that can do to an intelligent mind. All she could do was create an endless bubble map that branched out like a cancer of how Edith could strike her dead right here and now. There was no way to confirm if this even *was* Edith. All she knew was that this wasn't the body Suma and the guard were about to discover along with Penelope in the basement. Wrapped up in the most condemning fashion.

Harriet could only hear Emberly continuing to stall them in hopes for something to come along to distract them entirely from the course of searching that floor. She couldn't meet her eyes but shook like a leaf as Edith crept closer.

Hands clasped behind her back, Edith bent down to

inspect her closely like a museum artifact. Even though she was a millimeter from Harriet's ear, she hardly heard Edith say, "I think I like—"

"NO, DON'T!" Emberly howled from down below.

Edith led the way as they bolted downstairs to find the door open and everyone inside the room consumed with darkness.

They arrived, and all the shouting voices echoed in the room, drowning out whatever anyone was saying as Suma reached for the light.

The room fell completely silent.

Chapter Forty-Two

To everyone else's astonishment, the room contained nothing beyond the dirt they expected and the circuit breaker. Suma whipped her head up, down, and around, searching for whatever had caused Emberly to act out. But there was nothing. The guard watched us slowly, then shifted his flashlight to the ceiling and found, again, nothing.

Suma rolled her eyes. "Couldn't you have used that from the beginning?"

Not giving him time to answer the rhetorical jab, she turned her attention elsewhere.

"Well, where's the pot, Miss Emberly?" Suma asked, scanning the floor as if it might materialize at her feet.

"I—erm—I—I was just kidding! Wanted to get you riled up, make you think you were about to make a big bust. Surprise!"

"Seriously? Emberly, don't play with me tonight."

"Yeah, no, it's just a joke!" She gestured around the empty room. "As you can see—no drugs." Her voice cracking at the end.

Suma responded with a suspicious hum.

Emberly turned to me, dumbfounded, expecting I had all the answers. Because I did. Meanwhile, Harriet's brows were pinched together—her beautiful analytical mind spinning through problems and outcomes in microseconds. Nothing like Sylvia's. Sylvia would've caved by now.

I had to commend Emberly—she tried to take the fall.

Maybe she wasn't as bad as I thought. Sylvia had a talent for bringing out the worst in people. And it brings me a strange warmth to say she *had*.

I can talk about her now like a distant beloved—one who left too soon.

Now that she's gone, I can see my own mistakes.

I wasn't present enough.

And I couldn't let Harriet take the fall for something that was never hers to carry.

Harriet tried to heal me. Well—Hannah, technically—but still, me. Thank Discordia she played her role well enough to stay under the radar. Harriet might be a little freak, but she needs to be protected.

Emberly wasn't damned when she tortured Hannah. She damned herself when she learned everything about me and still chose to follow an idiot. And when I saw them kiss at dinner, loving each other in front of me—I wanted both of them to suffer.

She protected Harriet, yes. But she wasn't kind. Not like Harry. Still, that alone is why I was willing to make a truce. Now that we all live together.

I'm sure over time, we can learn new versions of each

other while trying to avoid being murdered or betrayed by each other.

Suma looked to me like this was outside her control, and she didn't know how to remedy the scene on display for a new student, "I'm sorry, Edith, for all this on your first night. Very on brand for this place, though." She let out a huff and turned off the light above her. Ushering everyone out, she said, "I don't know what you're on, Miss Emberly, but I don't think it's smart to lie about committing a crime when you haven't. A real police officer wouldn't take that so lightly. Think about that next time you wish to pull such pranks."

"My bad. It was the wrong timing, Suma." She pouted, feigning childishness. "I'm *sowwy*. Please forgive me."

Suma ruffled her hair and laughed it off, "Alright, alright, TED talk over."

Tapping the guard on the shoulder looked like Suma had broken him out of his fluoride stare. "Come on, Bill, let's just head back. I'm tired."

He hummed in agreement and walked toward the golf cart parked on the main road. Suma followed and turned to us at the last second.

"Y'all be good to Edith now," she said, pointing with her clipboard.

"We will! Thank you!" Emberly called after her.

As the golf cart disappeared into the darkness and the hum of the engine receded, we remained there, frozen.

Harry took the first step. The cold air cutting so clean it carried every crunch of gravel—each one too crisp to ignore. Emberly's shoulders dropped slightly, like she'd dodged a bullet that still came close enough to graze her.

Before I could step through, Emberly grabbed me by the collar with both hands and slammed my back into the brick wall.

"Who the *fuck* are you?"

I hissed, "You know who I am. *You're* the one who killed me."

"Stop playing games. If you're Edith, then *who the fuck was she?*"

"She wasn't real." I locked eyes with her and smiled wide—gumline to gumline. "But *I* am."

Tears welled up in Emberly's eyes. Her teeth clenched. "*Where* the fuck are they?"

"Who, exactly?" I tilted my head, innocent.

"You know where Sylvia is." When I didn't answer she slapped me hard across the face. Blood flaked off her hand.

"Is this some kind of sick prank?"

That made me giggle.

She slammed me again. When I looked up, Harriet stood in the doorway, horrified. I gave her my best smile and winked.

She bolted upstairs, letting the kitchen screen door slam behind her.

Emberly tried again, voice trembling, "Where the *fuck* is she?"

"Can't you tell?" I spread my arms wide, displaying my blood-soaked clothing. "I'm *wearing* her."

She dropped me like I was on fire. Backed away, staring at her trembling hands, now sticky with Sylvia's blood. She looked as though she might implode.

She collapsed to the ground, curling into herself.

I sat on the bottom step as she said, "What the fuck is going on…"

Giving her a double tap on the shoulder, I said, "Let's chat, Em."

Chapter Forty-Three

Gathered at the table. Emberly and Harriet took their seat on one side. Me on the other.

Harriet twiddled her fingers under the table, shoulders hunched. "So… you killed Syl. And somehow managed to get rid of the bodies for us?"

"Correct." I sat with perfect posture, hands folded neatly.

"And that's her blood all over you. *Right now.*"

"Yes." I hissed the word.

Harriet shook. Her chair rattled. "And now you live here."

"With *you*, specifically."

"Me?" Harriet started to dissociate.

"You have an empty bed in a two-person room. It wasn't hard to request—since it was already available." I leaned back, tilting the chair and lacing my fingers behind my head, grinning. "Any other statement-questions?"

Emberly looked murderous. Her face flushed dark red. "No. You can fucking stay in the closet for all I care. But *not* with Harry. No. *No fucking way*. I'm not letting that happen."

"There *is* a way. And I did it." I leaned forward, my tone dropping into something serious. "Look—I want us all to get along."

Emberly let out a scoffing laugh. "Right. Yeah. No one's making it to tomorrow if *you're* in this house. I'll never sleep again."

"I see your point. But we're not victims here. We could use this alliance to our advantage."

"What the fuck does that even *mean*?" Emberly shot up, pacing. She rubbed the tension from her forehead. "You really expect us to believe you disposed of everything—*everyone*—without a trace, while you're still *covered* in drying blood? And you don't even *itch*?"

She shook her head, losing it.

"You expect us to believe we're good? That you don't plan to kill us or frame us? All because you *want* to be friends with the people who murdered—who was it again?"

"Her name was Hannah."

"Hannah. Who was posing as *you*. No. I don't trust you for a *second*."

"Then you'll end up like Syl. Or—I'll leak everything. Tell me, Emberly, how would your family and friends on Fifth Avenue feel when they discover what you've done? Didn't they threaten to cut you off over the last incident?"

Emberly's mouth was contorting, "How the *fuck* do you know that?"

Ignoring the question, "Way I see it, you have two choices. From here, you accept me as I come to you, trying to make amends for things that weren't your fault. It's hunt or be hunted, and I think we would make *great* hunters together rather than hunting each other. Whether you think so or not, *I let you* survive for a reason. So, we should live. We chose this path and need to protect one another now because, on the other end, you could discover the cost of inaction. You kick me out now, and you will never know peace. I'll drag your asses down for everything you did. No scratch off my back. Or…"

I leaned in, deadly calm.

"…I could just kill you. Your choice."

I waited. Patiently.

Eventually, they nodded. Complacent. Like they'd done with Syl.

"Good."

Harriet opened her mouth. "Yes, Harry?"

Color bloomed in her cheeks from the use of her nickname.

"How'd you do it?" she asked. "How'd you get the bodies out—by yourself?"

I stood, scraping my chair loudly. "I just took them. Not hard when you're always watching the front door."

They realized then how little they'd known. The plan they thought they'd created—it was always mine.

"You knew…" Harriet whispered.

"Everything. Always. What—did you really think Sylvia Harrington was in control? That she was just some girl, helpless in her own life? Cute. Naive, really."

I laughed as I leaned on the table. "If you're worried about sleep, rest easy in the comfort of knowing I'm too exhausted to kill anyone else tonight. It's been a long time coming, so I'm going to shower and move my shit into Harry's."

Emberly followed me to the stairs, "Hey."

Only when I looked back did she ask, "So, you're just going to bury this?"

I twisted toward her, one hand on the banister. "Like the rest."

Then I walked off to shower, leaving Emberly frozen, still trying to unpack the weight of what I'd said.

At the top, I caught Harriet's eyes. She was crying. And when Emberly moved to comfort her, Harriet recoiled, shoving her hand away.

"No."

"Alright. Fine. You're crying. I'm worried. What's on your mind?"

"Nothing. I'm good. I'm just… processing."

Chapter Forty-Four

This was my home now. I'd solidified my place in this house full of people who intended to leave me to be eaten by bugs. Now, I needed a fucking shower.

No matter how giddy I felt about being accepted—whether through fear or otherwise—I fucking did it.

Standing beneath the near-boiling water, I let the tears stream down my face. I didn't want to lose the sensation of being wrapped in Sylvia. The blood had long since dried, but I didn't care. I would've worn it forever. A small piece of me ached as I let it wash down the drain, but I knew I'd never really lose her. Sylvia would always be with me, one way or another.

They say when people die, their soul's often linger—attending their own funerals, watching the world unravel after they leave. I lost myself in the fantasy of Sylvia standing just outside the shower curtain, waiting for me. There wouldn't be a funeral, but I liked to imagine her soul tethered to mine for eternity. God, what a sight it would be—her essence trapped for years, unable to escape me. I plan to make death insufferable for her.

Fuck, this is the best day of my life.

When the water began to cool, I got out and opened the window. The full moon beckoned me, just as it had for ages. I couldn't remember the last time I'd slept indoors. Sure, I could have slept in my car—but where's the thrill in that? What's the point of the hunt if you don't fight for your life a little along the way?

After standing at the open window air-drying, I didn't bother with a towel. I stepped out of the bathroom completely bare.

Harriet stood at the top of the stairs, watching the door.

She didn't flinch at my nakedness. She just stood there, statuesque in the light and steam filtering from the bathroom.

"Would you mind washing a load of towels?" I asked. "I would, but—" I trailed off, the silence pulling taut between us. Her expression didn't shift. It drove me crazy. "—only if you don't mind."

She responded with a curt "Hm."

"I'm going to get dressed, roomie." I pointed toward the guest room Hannah had barely inhabited. I kept my chin high and gave her my best toffee-eyed stare before breaking eye contact and closing the door behind me.

They'll adjust. Give them time. I kept reminding myself it doesn't matter—they can't do anything. I'm here to stay.

I flopped down on the bed.

It's not like I *wanted* to room with Harriet. It was just my only option. Penelope's room had been paid for as a single, and the guest room Hannah stayed in wasn't an official dorm room. Every move had to seem deliberate.

Honestly, I didn't think I'd make it this far. Thought I'd be either arrested or dead by now. The cops should've been called ages ago. But everyone on this fucking planet is egocentric and oblivious. Syl was right when she said women can hide in plain sight.

My clothes felt a little tight, but I didn't give a fuck. I kicked my feet around on the bed, barely containing my giggles.

When I heard Emberly shut and lock her door, I knew she wouldn't come out again tonight. Harriet was downstairs, good. I wanted a cup of tea after watching everyone else drink theirs. Fate willing, Harriet still had some of that psychedelic shit around. After I kept her sober, I knew Hannah was probably having the time of her life.

I took the servant's stairs, grabbed the kettle, and set it on the stove. Looking out the window, I stared at the lot out back, imagining what it all looked like from their perspective.

This wasn't a dream. I was making tea. Drinking from *their* cups. Whatever the fuck I wanted.

Wandering through the dining room into the living room, I caught Harriet's reflection in the bay window—another textbook cradling her focus. Maybe this was her way of playing dead.

She couldn't hide from me.

"Tea?" I asked.

Harriet looked up warily.

I bent down until I was eye level. "Only *one* of us is good at funny tricks with tea." I tried to speak gently. Her features softened, ever so slightly. It was working.

"You have it every night," I added. "Don't break the routine just because of me."

Her skin shifted from warm pale to a bluish hue. The realization that she had been *seen*—truly perceived—must have chilled her blood.

"You're a floral woman, right?" I tapped her shoulder twice. "I'm sure I'll find something for the two of us."

I could practically *hear* her gulp as I returned to the kitchen.

The kettle whistled, shrill and horrible. I loved it.

Harriet tried to control every movement, every expression, as I handed her the amber liquid in her favorite teacup and saucer.

I grabbed Penelope's mug that Sylvia coveted and plopped down on the couch with Alain Fournier's *Le Grand Meaulnes*.

Nestled in our spots in the living room, we shared cups of ethereal tea in silence, broken only by the soft sounds of sipping. As we immersed ourselves in our books, we'd occasionally glance over the pages at each other, an exchange that felt both cautious and familiar. Unspoken doubts and a silent pact. A mutual understanding that held us in place until the first light of dawn crept through the windows.